THE RELUCTANT PLAYERS

By

Ron Barker

Dedicated to all of those who want to write a book.

Also to my mom
for being my editor and to my wife for creating the cover.

CHAPTER ONE

As the plane began its descent, Lisa Lasham put away her notebook and sat back in her seat looking relaxed and confident. Lisa was just 26 years old and stood five foot ten. She wasn't what one would call attractive. She had short hair that looked like it had been cut by someone one who suffered from the shakes. Her overbite made her front lip stick out just enough to be noticeable. She had dated a little in college, but never had a serious boyfriend.

Lisa threw herself into her work and had recently completed her first year of employment at the National Collegiate Athletic Association (NCAA) as an assistant director of enforcement. She loved the authority that her job gave her. It took her mind off of her unsuccessful personal life, at least unsuccessful in her mother's mind. Her mother wanted grandkids and Lisa was nowhere close to providing any.

At that moment Lisa was on her way to another school to investigate allegations of more violations of NCAA rules. She loved conducting investigations, interviewing student-athletes and their coaches. She would never admit this out loud, but if the truth were to be known, Lisa loved the sense of power she felt arriving on campus. People treated her with respect and at times with fear. Lisa knew that came with the position, but she liked being the person in charge, especially when dealing with powerful football or basketball coaches.

Like many others on the enforcement staff, Lisa was a huge sports fan. She had attended Duke University as an undergrad playing on the volleyball team then attended the University of Kansas for law school. She had graduated in the middle of her class and went to work as an assistant district attorney in Kansas. She realized quickly that she didn't enjoy being an ADA so she began exploring other options.

A friend had mentioned that the NCAA enforcement staff was hiring. Lisa was a KU and Duke basketball fan, but didn't think she knew enough about sports to work at the NCAA. She hesitantly sent a resume and application for the job. Surprisingly she had gotten a call, been flown to Indianapolis for an interview and been hired to work in enforcement.

Thinking back over her first few weeks she remembered how confused she had been by all she had to know and comprehend. She tried to learn the litany of NCAA rules, but one of the other staff members told her that she just needed to get a handle on the basics, the rest would come over time.

"You only need to know enough to be able to ask questions then bring the information back to the mother ship for a review," she had been told. As she gained more knowledge of NCAA rules and procedures she got better at her job, but she now understood that one didn't have to be an expert at NCAA rules to work in enforcement. You just needed to know what areas to explore during interviews as well as what questions might lead to additional information. The rules changed so quickly it was hard to keep up!

Lisa had studied hard during her first month, often spending ten to twelve hours at the office. She took home more material to read and poured over past case files. Finally the day had arrived when she went on her training trip. Sitting in on interviews with a seasoned investigator, Lisa had been surprised to find out that the investigator she had been paired up with didn't seem to be very good at asking questions. She had thought that many of the questions could have been phrased better or been asked more clearly. That gave her additional confidence that she would be fine when she was finally unleashed to investigate on her own.

She had trained for a short period, then been given her own first small case. She had investigated, interviewed, chased down information then run the whole thing by her supervisor who had praised her for her hard work. No hearing was needed on that particular case, but violations had been uncovered and reported officially to the NCAA.

Now that Lisa was beginning her second year on the job she felt like she was one of the seasoned investigators and had full confidence in her abilities. The case she was now working on was very interesting. A basketball coach had hired a man who had been employed as a junior college basketball coach to be his assistant coach. The man had two very good players on his junior college team and they followed their coach to the four-year school. Bringing players with you to a new job wasn't in and of itself a violation of

NCAA rules, but the employment could not be conditioned upon bringing players with you to the new job.

Lisa had been told that proving this type of case was one of the hardest things to do because usually there was nothing in writing that would prove that a person was hired only if he brought players with him. It also wasn't in anyone's best interest to admit that some type of agreement had been in place prior to the actual employment. Proving this agreement was in place would only happen if someone admitted it in an interview.

The information had come in over the NCAA phone lines from a source who wished to remain anonymous. The source had told Lisa that everyone knew the agreement was in place prior to the coach being hired. The junior college coach would only get the assistant coaching job if he delivered the two players who had starred for him at the junior college. The informant also said the players weren't happy about the arrangement because they didn't like the coach very much.

Lisa pondered over that for a moment. If the players didn't like the junior college coach, there was nothing, as far as she could see, that forced them to go with their JC coach to the four-year school. That made no sense to her as she thought about it. That would have to be an area she explored during the investigation.

To make matters even more interesting, the assistant coach had worked at another university years ago and had been charged and found guilty in a prior NCAA case. He had been fired from his employment only to find a job at the junior college. Now the same person was back on the NCAA radar in this new case. Coincidence? Lisa didn't believe in coincidences.

Lisa knew this would be a tough case to prove, but if she was somehow able to get enough proof to take it to the NCAA Committee on Infractions it would continue to cement her reputation as one of the up and comers on the enforcement staff. On the other hand, she had very little to lose if she wasn't able to get anything that would constitute proof in this case because these types of cases are so hard to prove by their very nature.

All of this rolled around Lisa's mind as she sat back in her seat on the plane. She loved the travel, loved being around sports, loved the reactions of her friends when she told them she worked on the NCAA enforcement staff. The money wasn't great, but it was good enough for now. She had dreams for her future, this current job was a stepping-stone to greater things, she was sure!

The plane landed, Lisa grabbed her carry-on from the overhead bin following the other passengers off of the plane. As she followed the signs to the rental car counter she reflected on how this job allowed her to see many parts of the United States she would not otherwise get to visit. Lisa got her rental car, input the location of the hotel into her GPS then drove the 18 miles to her Marriott hotel. She always stayed in the Marriott chain when possible because she was building her frequent flyer points and hotel points with an eye towards a future vacation in Europe in another year or two.

Upon arrival at the hotel, Lisa checked in, got her room key and trudged slowly to her room. People thought travel was glamorous, but the rooms all looked the same, the flights took a toll on your body. Lisa had only been doing it for a year, but she had already experienced the sensation of forgetting which rental car was hers and which room number she was in. Upon arriving to her room, Lisa unpacked her bags. This room looked the same as the last one and the one before that. Lisa was on the road about 100 days a year so she spent a lot of time in hotel rooms. She quickly changed clothes and headed to the workout room to get in an hour on the treadmill.

Later that evening Lisa went to a chain restaurant for dinner. She always brought a book to read during dinner. At first she had been very uncomfortable dining alone, but she had grown used to it. Now she read her book while waiting for her food. After dinner she went back to the hotel, read up on her notes regarding the case and prepared to arrive on campus the next day.

The following morning Lisa awoke early, read her USA Today newspaper spending most of her time in the sports section. Her name had once appeared in the paper in connection with an investigation she had been working on. She had purchased 25 copies of the paper and sent them to her family and friends. That had been very exciting for her. If she had really stopped to think about it, she might have seen that she was too interested in having her name known, maybe her ego was a little too big, but she didn't pause for much introspection at this point in her life. She wanted glory and money, most of all she wanted to win.

She got in her car and drove to campus. One of the things she had learned in her first year on the job is that parking is at a premium on almost every campus in the United States. An attorney for one school in the Southeastern Conference had told her to park then bring any tickets she got to him. He said it would be easier to get the ticket taken away than it was to get her a parking pass.

For her current assignment at Grand Central State, Lisa had spoken with the compliance director who had sent her a parking pass. She hung it from her mirror as she exited the car. She gathered her materials from the back seat, locked the car, then headed towards the athletics staff offices. As she neared the building a young man about 30 years old walked towards her.

"Are you Lisa?" he asked. She told him she was. He introduced himself as Shawn Morgan and told her he was the compliance director at Grand Central State. They shook hands then Shawn directed her to a building.

"We're going to meet the president of the university who would like to speak with you for a few moments then we'll head down to the athletics building."

Lisa responded that would be fine, but asked Shawn why the president wanted to speak with her. Lisa found that some of the university presidents or chancellors wanted to be involved or at least know what was going on, others wanted nothing to do with the investigation leaving it to the athletics staff. Some enforcement staff members at the NCAA thought the president's involvement was a good sign that the school was taking the investigation seriously. Lisa's experience had been that some of the presidents took it seriously, others wanted to try to intimidate the NCAA representative, while others felt they should greet the NCAA, but then wanted to get far away from the investigation. Lisa had learned not to form any opinions going in.

They walked into the president's office. A man about 6'4" stood to greet them. "Well little lady, welcome to Grand Central State! I'm Kevin Scott, the president here. We take this matter very seriously and I want you to know we'll do our best to assist your investigation."

Lisa didn't take too well to being called little lady. She immediately wanted to take this large man down a peg. She tried not to show her irritation as she shook his hand.

"The NCAA will try to work with the university to see if there are any problems and address those problems in the most judicial manner," Lisa replied.

President Scott smiled. "Most judicial manner? That doesn't sound very pleasant," he laughed.

Lisa had worked with a few of these middle-sized schools before. They weren't accustomed to NCAA investigators poking their noses into school business. They usually couldn't afford to hire one of the four or five attorneys who specialized in NCAA matters. Often, they would appoint an attorney from the school to represent them during the investigation. Lisa loved when that happened because the attorneys would have no idea what the NCAA process entailed. The attorneys would fall back on legal training and anyone well versed in NCAA investigations knew that they were very different from a regular legal hearing.

Lisa visited with the president for a few minutes then explained quickly that she was on campus to conduct some interviews to determine whether or not a problem even existed. She liked to put the other party at ease. She explained that once she conducted these first interviews, she would take the information back to Indianapolis where a group would decide whether more interviews were needed.

"That sounds fine to me," president Scott responded. "Let me know if there is anything that you need. I trust that our athletics officials will assist you as I've instructed."

With that he dismissed Lisa from his office. Shawn, who had been waiting outside in the lobby, stood. "Follow me, we'll head down to the athletics building."

As Lisa walked with Shawn she viewed the campus. It was a large campus with reflective ponds and greenbelts that made it seem very spread out. Another thing Lisa had learned from her time at the NCAA is that there were some very beautiful college campuses across the U.S. and Grand Central State University was another one of those. She had barely heard of Grand Central State University (GCSU). GCSU had made the NCAA basketball tournament the previous year, but that was the first time. They had never come close to making the tournament before that so it was big news locally. GCSU didn't have a football program so it wasn't in the national news often.

Lisa had done some research prior to coming on campus. She found out that GCSU had roughly 18,000 students enrolled in the current term. There was a faculty-to-student ratio of about 1-19. GCSU was founded in the late 1800s to teach agriculture, but now offered a wide range of degrees in agricultural and environmental sciences as well as business, education and engineering. It had masters and doctoral programs in agricultural sciences as well as engineering.

GCSU had been a division II school within the NCAA until ten years ago when it could no longer pass up the NCAA basketball money so the administration upgraded just enough to be classified as division I and be eligible for the NCAA Division I basketball tournament or what is commonly referred to as March Madness.

Lisa had seen this before, a smaller school wanted to cash in on the big basketball tournament money so they put in just enough effort to qualify then weren't able to keep up with the competition. Some schools, with good leadership, realized this and dropped back down to division II. Others hired circumspect individuals to become involved with the basketball program as head or assistant coaches. Other than a big football program that cost a lot to run, basketball was where the money was. As a result, the reputation of the sport of basketball continued to suffer with individuals who should never have been put in positions of leadership with young men. Lisa had often wondered where the presidents of the universities were when these hires were made. At least, she reasoned, it kept her busy at work!

As she walked with Shawn she tried to engage him in conversation. "So Shawn, how long have you been at GCSU?" Lisa asked.

"I'm beginning my sixth year in compliance here," Shawn answered. "I started as an intern, but then got the full-time job when my predecessor moved on to a bigger school."

"Are you hoping to do the same?" Lisa questioned.

"Oh no, I love it here," Shawn replied. "I was born here, went to school here and my parents and siblings all live within 30 minutes. I know I could make more money somewhere else, but money isn't everything! Family is much more important to me."

Even though Lisa thought he was crazy to settle for a little school like GCSU, she found herself liking Shawn. She hoped her investigation wouldn't cause him any problems with his job, but often the compliance person ended up as the scapegoat after an investigation was completed. The athletics directors (ADs) were the boss, but most ADs considered compliance a necessary evil and didn't get nearly involved enough in supporting the compliance staff or provide necessary resources. When problems hit, the compliance staff often was blamed.

Shawn continued talking "we're going to the AD's office. Mike Love is our athletics director. He has been here for five years and has done a tremendous job bringing in greater resources. He brought in over 3 million dollars in donations last year."

Lisa walked along with Shawn. She found that she could get a lot of information in these informal conversations before or in between the actual interviews.

"How is Mike Love when it comes to compliance?" Lisa asked. "Does he have your back when a coach gets upset?"

"Oh, pretty much. Occasionally a coach will disagree with my interpretation of a rule and might go to Mike, but Mike will talk to me privately to see if there is a way to work it out to make the coach happier. He never does it in front of the coach."

Lisa didn't like the sound of that, but she let it pass. They arrived at the athletics building. Shawn introduced Lisa to Mike Love who invited her into his office. Shawn joined them for the discussion.

"We are going to fully cooperate with your investigation," Mike Love began. "Whatever you need, Shawn will provide it to you. Just between the three of us, I'm not happy with the direction of the men's basketball coaching staff. If they have done something wrong we want to help you uncover it and then we'll deal with it. If the NCAA provides some type of penalty we'll abide by it and use that in our decision regarding how to handle things internally."

Lisa thanked Love for his attitude and then said she was ready to begin her interviews. As she rose to leave, Love said there was one other item. At that specific moment a man walked into the office.

"This is Matt Colter," Love explained. "He will be acting on behalf of the university during the investigation."

Lisa turned to see a nice looking man in his early 30s smiling at her. He put forth his hand to offer it to Lisa while saying "Hi, I'm Matt Colter. I formally worked at the NCAA in enforcement, now I work with schools, pleased to meet you!"

CHAPTER TWO

"You worked in enforcement at the NCAA?" Lisa asked. She had been unprepared for GCSU to have someone representing them at the interviews other than the compliance officer or maybe a campus attorney. Having someone experienced in NCAA enforcement matters changed everything and she knew that she better be on her toes.

"Yes," Matt replied. "I was there for a couple of years then left to go out on my own." He left it at that so Lisa didn't ask any further questions. She was anxious to learn a little about him. Would he fight her every step of the way? If he worked at the NCAA in enforcement, perhaps he would be helpful to her. She would watch him carefully.

"I will interview the coaches then figure out where we go from there", Lisa stated. "Feel free to ask any questions you may have as we go along."

Shawn led everyone to a conference room. Lisa sat on one side of the table, Shawn and Matt sat on the other. Lisa began unpacking, pulling notebooks and pens out along with a digital recorder. Shawn hadn't been a part of this before so he hadn't brought anything with him, but Lisa and Matt both had a regular routine that anyone observing would have noticed.

Lisa put the recorder front and center along with several forms that she would have each interviewee sign. She had folders full of notes and documents that she kept covered. She also pulled out a large diet Dr. Pepper, which she drank during each interview.

Matt on the other hand, had his digital recorder, a notebook and pen. He sat and waited for Lisa to be ready. Shawn didn't know what he was supposed to do, but Matt told him he should sit in on the interviews.

First up to be interviewed was head basketball coach Ned McEnroe. Ned came into the room, greeted Shawn with a familiar wave then asked where he should sit. Lisa told him he should sit at the head of the table.

Ned McEnroe was mid 60s, had silver hair and appeared to be in very good shape. If you had to use one word to describe him it would have been smooth. He just seemed to be what every man in his 60s would want to be. Ned had coached at a number of schools. He had a good run with a larger school for about ten years then left for a higher paying job, where he failed miserably. GCSU had hired him on his downward slide looking to capitalize on his name and the success he had earlier while not having to fork out the big bucks that McEnroe would have commanded years earlier.

It had not gone well at the beginning. GCSU had lost big during Ned's first two years. The administration quickly came to the realization that Ned didn't have the energy and possibly the desire to recruit at the level needed to achieve any success. Ned had hired an assistant coach who recruited a few good players then they had hired another assistant coach from the junior college ranks who brought two pretty good players with him. That had lead to their NCAA tournament appearance the previous year where they had lost in the fist round.

McEnroe looked anxious as the interview began. Lisa explained that the NCAA had a number of procedures it needed to follow so once she turned on her recorder she would walk through the formalities before beginning the actual interview. Then she slipped in "you don't mind if I record do you?" to McEnroe.

McEnroe mumbled something then shook his head indicating that he didn't mind. Lisa liked doing it that way because it really was to everyone's benefit if she was permitted to record. She would have an accurate record of what was said, the interviewee would be able to refute any claims the NCAA might make against him or her by going to the recording to see exactly what was said. Every once in a while someone objected to the recording so Lisa would have to take much more diligent notes. With the recording she would take it back to the office and have a staff member transcribe the recording.

Matt introduced himself to McEnroe and explained that he was representing GCSU. "You need to remember that I represent the school, not you. I will try to assist and help where possible, but don't ever forget that I am here to represent the school. At any point should you feel you need an attorney you should stop the interview and ask for time to get an attorney".

Ned indicated that he understood. Matt noticed that Lisa didn't seem to like him taking charge for a few moments. He stored that away for later use.

Lisa turned on the recorder as she began. Matt Colter did the same with his recorder. Lisa provided the date and location of the interview, then explained that Coach McEnroe had read through the form explaining the relevant bylaws that obligated him to be truthful and forthcoming during the interview. Coach McEnroe acknowledged that what Lisa was saying was true, then she had him sign and date the form. He acknowledged that he had given his permission to be recorded and acknowledged that he knew he had the right to an attorney, but had chosen to proceed without an attorney present. Lisa then had each person in the room identify himself for purposes of the recording. After each person identified himself by name and title they were ready to begin.

Lisa had McEnroe outline his coaching history by identifying each location where he had worked and for how long he had been there. McEnroe walked through the past forty years of his life finishing with his current job at GCSU as the head coach.

Matt Colter noticed that McEnroe's hands were shaking as he spoke. At first he thought McEnroe might be nervous, but soon started seeing a small tremor and movement with his arms and legs as well. Colter thought that McEnroe might be in the early stages of Parkinson's disease. He made a note to try to ease McEnroe's stress when possible.

Once McEnroe concluded his job history Lisa asked him to give a brief overview of his duties as head coach at GCSU. McEnroe looked at her like he didn't understand the question.

"Do you want me to tell you everything I do every day or just a quick recap. I mean I could start talking and go until next week trying to tell you everything a head coach does in his job, but I guess I oversee everything involved with the men's basketball program, from on-court coaching, to recruiting to scouting to meeting with boosters to raising funds to media interviews and on and on. I'm not sure how much you want me to say."

"That is fine," Lisa responded. "I guess I'm just trying to see if there is anything of significance that you delegate to your assistants."

"Like what for example?" McEnroe asked.

"Oh, I don't know, " Lisa answered. "I've heard some coaches don't like to recruit so they leave it up to their assistants. Others don't want to watch film of opponents. Is there anything that you aren't involved with that maybe other head coaches do?"

McEnroe thought about it for a moment then shook his head. "No, I don't think there is anything like that. I probably let my assistants do more of the face to face dealings with recruits and their families, but I'm still involved."

"Okay that is good for now," Lisa responded. "Let's talk about how you came to hire your assistant coaches. Explain the steps you take to identify and hire the right people."

McEnroe began by telling the group how coaches became acquainted with each other through camps, clinics and other activities. He had met hundreds of coaches through his years and had worked with many.

"But how did you go about hiring your two assistants?" Lisa asked. "Let's start with Randy Culp first. I see by the media guide that he is your first assistant. How did you decide to hire him?"

"Well I knew Randy's father years ago. When I took the job at my prior school I hired Randy as the Director of Basketball Operations. I knew he wanted to get into coaching and this was a way for him to get his foot in the door. He did a good job there so when I took the job at GCSU I brought Randy with me. I felt he was ready to be an assistant coach at this level."

"Great, so how did you come to hire your second assistant, let's see uhm" Lisa thumbed through the media guide she had brought with her. "Here it is, how did you come to hire Ken Reid? Did you have a prior relationship with him?"

Matt knew that Lisa was very well aware of what Ken Reid's name was. She was trying to act nonchalant, but Ken Reid was the main focus of the investigation and Lisa knew his name without looking for it in the media guide. Matt always liked to watch the habits of the NCAA investigators. He kept notes on each one so he knew their tendencies better than they did. Lisa was new to him, but he was starting his file already.

"No, I had never heard of him," McEnroe explained. "My first year here we had Marvin Bennett as the second assistant, but he left in the middle of the year for personal reasons. We never really replaced him, but Randy Culp told me he knew of a JC basketball coach he thought would fit in nicely here."

Lisa thought about this for a minute. Then she asked her question, "so Randy Culp was the person who hired Ken Reid?"

McEnroe laughed, "no, I hire my assistants, but Randy suggested him. I guess you could say he brought Ken to my attention."

From time to time Lisa would glance over at Matt. She didn't know why, but having him sitting there disturbed her for some reason. Matt hadn't spoken, but was taking notes and smiling at McEnroe as he spoke. McEnroe, more often than not, would direct his answers to Matt instead of to her. She decided that might be what was bothering her. She would have to fix that.

"So Coach McEnroe, what were the things you liked about Ken Reid?"

McEnroe thought for a moment then said "well he had worked at a Division I school before, his junior college team had been very successful and..."

Lisa saw McEnroe looking at Matt again so she interrupted, "Coach McEnroe, I'm the one asking you questions. It would be nice if you responded to me instead of directing your answers to Mr. Colter".

McEnroe looked startled. Matt held in his smile. He knew he had gotten to Lisa without doing anything. It was such a trivial issue, but Matt knew that often, the enforcement staff member wouldn't be comfortable with someone who didn't shrink in fear. He liked to see how the enforcement staff member acted early on in an investigation. He had done nothing to try to rankle her. She wanted to be important and that was useful information to have going forward.

McEnroe apologized then continued answering while looking directly at Lisa, "As I was saying, Ken Reid had been successful at the junior college ranks, he had already recruited at a division I NCAA school and I thought he was a good fit for our program."

"Did you know he had a couple of good players at his junior college that would most likely come with him to GCSU if you hired him?"

"Did I know he had a couple of good players at the JC? Yes. Did I know they would come with him if we hired him? I hoped they would, but I don't think we knew for sure."

Lisa thought about that then asked her next question, "If the two players had not come with Ken Reid would you still have hired him?"

"I don't think we will ever know for sure because they did come with him," McEnroe replied. "We can talk all day long about what might have happened, but the bottom line is we hired Ken Reid and the two players did come with him."

Lisa tried another tack, "Let me ask this in a different way. Did you ever tell Ken Reid that he would only be hired if the two players came with him?"

McEnroe could have just said no, but he was trying to be honest. "Let me see if I can answer this as truthfully as possible."

"That's always a good approach," Matt joked.

McEnroe looked over at Matt and smiled back, but then he remembered to look at Lisa. "I never told Ken that he would only be hired if he brought the players with him. I think he understood that part of the reason he was being hired was because he was affiliated with the players, but I don't think we ever told him his hiring was conditioned upon bringing the two players."

Lisa was more confused than before. She just wanted a straight answer, but wasn't getting one. "Would Ken Reid have been working for you if the two players had gone elsewhere?"

"But they did come here so I can't answer that question. It is purely hypothetical," McEnroe smiled.

Matt could tell Lisa was frustrated, but he couldn't help, but laugh a little. These investigations always threw something new at you. It would have been so simple for McEnroe to just say he would have hired Reid no matter what, but he wasn't saying that. He really wasn't answering the question and Matt could see no reason why he wouldn't just give a straight answer. Matt thought it was funny to watch Lisa's frustration.

McEnroe also realized that the NCAA rep was getting upset with him. He tried again, "knowing that Ken Reid had two good players certainly pushed him to the top of the list when looking for a new assistant. If he didn't have those two good players I don't know if he would have been at the top of my list, but I did know he had two good players so that moved him up. I didn't know for sure we would get them when we agreed to hire Ken, but we hoped we would and that definitely influenced our decision. Is that good enough?"

Lisa sighed then said "it will have to be for now."

This was the whole crux of the case and Lisa didn't think she had enough proof that a violation had been committed. She would keep plugging away by talking to others, but she was quickly realizing why these types of cases were the most difficult to prove.

"So once Ken Reid came, how long before you found out that the two young players would be attending GCSU?"

"Oh, I'm not sure exactly when I knew. Ken and Randy recruited the two players from Ken's junior college. They could both tell you the time frame much better than I could, but at some point I became aware that both would be attending GCSU and playing for us."

"And did that excite you?", Lisa asked.

"Of course it did," McEnroe responded. "They were both good players, better than the returning players we had. I thought both would not only contribute, but most likely be starting for us that year and I was right. One became all conference and averaged 22 points a game, the other lead the team in assists. We finished first in our league and went to the NCAA tournament with them."

"Okay Coach McEnroe, that is enough for now. I'll probably want to speak with you again, but this is good for the first meeting."

Lisa concluded by reading the obligatory information, turned off her recorder and thanked McEnroe for meeting with her. McEnroe smiled and said "no problem, but could I ask a question?"

"Sure," Lisa replied.

"Have we done something wrong?"

Lisa often got these types of questions and had learned quickly how to respond. "We don't know the answer to that, which is why we come out to meet with people and ask questions. We'll figure it out and you'll be one of the first to know."

Matt couldn't help himself, he had to add "unless you never hear anything, that happens from time to time as well!"

Lisa didn't like that comment so she assured Coach McEnroe that she would personally talk to him once she had reached some type of conclusion. McEnroe thanked them both and exited the room quickly.

Lisa looked angrily at Matt, but Matt kept smiling as he turned to Shawn. "So who is next?"

Shawn said that Lisa had asked to speak with Randy Culp next. Lisa confirmed that so Shawn left to get Randy.

"I hope you know that I understand how difficult that NCAA enforcement job is," Matt said. "I may joke, but these are tough cases and I'll help to get to the bottom of this."

Lisa turned to him and said, "thanks for the offer, but I don't think I'll need your help."

CHAPTER THREE

"I haven't offended you, have I?" Matt asked.

"No, of course not. Why would I be offended when you imply that we aren't good at our job?" Lisa responded.

"Wait a second," Matt said. "I never said you weren't good at your job or that the NCAA wasn't good at investigations. There are times, however, when the enforcement staff doesn't follow through on keeping people informed."

Lisa didn't want to hear this. She was used to people ripping on the enforcement staff.

"How long did you work at the NCAA?" Lisa asked.

"Long enough to know it wasn't the right place for me," Matt laughed.

"Why was that? Was the work too difficult?" Lisa was trying to rile Matt a little. She didn't like his smug attitude.

Matt laughed again. Lisa thought he had a kind face when he laughed and she momentarily forgot that she was upset with him.

"The work wasn't too difficult, but you have to be a true believer to do a good job. I came to discover that I thought there was a lot of hypocrisy with what some of the leaders at the NCAA said and how they acted. I think the enforcement staff has a tough job to do, but some of the bylaws you are enforcing make no sense and when I came to that realization I also came to the realization that I needed to leave to be honest with myself. I left with no hard feelings."

"But then you began defending schools and working against us", Lisa really wanted to find out his motives.

"You see, that is part of the problem," Matt replied. "There shouldn't be an us vs. them mentality. Your job is to uncover the truth even if that information helps disprove the case and helps the school. There are too many in the enforcement staff who make it personal and try to bring down a school to enhance their own personal reputation. I fight that attitude. I want to uncover the truth. If someone cheated I want the cheaters to be punished.

However, if someone made an honest mistake, I want that person to learn from the mistake and move on better prepared to be successful in the future."

Lisa thought about that for a moment so Matt continued on.

"The enforcement staff supervisors don't do a good enough job reminding the staff that your job is to uncover the truth, no matter where it leads you. Too many think their job is to win the case at all costs. They fail to realize you get nothing more if you uncover things that hurt a school than if you uncover things that help a school. I've worked with too many enforcement staff people who don't realize that their job is to investigate and uncover truth. They want to get another scalp and build their own reputation. In their minds it is all about winning a case and that is the wrong attitude to have."

"And you don't think the NCAA wants to uncover the truth?" Lisa asked.

"The NCAA says they want that, but the reality is that many schools have to go through a hearing and get punished publicly for something that was nothing more than a mistake. The NCAA process often forgets to weigh intent. Then you get an overeager enforcement rep trying to make a name for him or herself and it is a bad combination. I want to help people and while there are many times you actually do help a school, I didn't feel like that was the focus, so I left."

"As easy as that, huh?" Lisa retorted.

"No, it wasn't easy. I really liked some of the people I worked with at the NCAA. As I've said, there are many dedicated enforcement staff members doing a good job, but the ones who are reckless, who don't do a good job, aren't weeded out. I thought long and hard about my decision, but I'm happy with what I am now doing."

At that moment Shawn returned. Walking in behind him was a five foot eight inch man in his mid 30s. He wore long baggy shorts and a baggy Tommy Bahama type shirt. His hair was shaggy and he wore sandals. He looked more like someone on vacation in Hawaii then he did an assistant basketball coach.

Shawn introduced him as Randy Culp, an assistant basketball coach at GCSU. They all shook hands then sat down. Lisa began her spiel about the process. Matt looked intently at Randy Culp. Mike Love, the AD, had mentioned to Matt that Love didn't particularly trust Randy Culp. Love used the words "smarmy" and "devious" when describing Culp. Love thought that if they had a problem, Culp was probably up to his elbows in it.

Matt didn't trust other people's opinions. Sure, he listened to them, but then he tried to understand for himself. He had to admit, Culp didn't give off a great first impression.

Lisa finished explaining the process and having Culp sign the forms agreeing to be honest and forthcoming during the interview. Culp had no problem with being recorded so the interview began.

Lisa danced around the perimeter for a while getting Culp's background and feeling him out for a bit. She finally got to the heart of the matter.

"When did you first meet Ken Reid and how long have you known him?"

Culp had a habit of grinning when he answered the questions. Matt didn't know if that came from nerves or was just a habit, but it didn't add to his likeability at all. Culp sat back and crossed his legs. He had left his sandals on the floor and his bare foot crossed over his knee.

"I first met Ken Reid about ten years ago or so when we were both assistant coaches at Southwest Metro State. Actually I was a graduate assistant coach and Ken was the Director of Basketball operations, but we were both heavily involved in coaching," Culp grinned. "That is one of the dumbest and most violated NCAA rules in the book. You guys only allow a school to have three assistant basketball coaches so schools hire people and give them titles like Director of Basketball Ops or Video Coordinator, while everyone knows they are actually coaches. What a charade!"

Lisa didn't like this and immediately got defensive. "If you know schools that are violating this rule, please enlighten me and I'll go investigate."

Matt inwardly groaned. This type of exchange happened in almost every case. There were rules that people violated, but they were hard to prove without being on campus or sitting in on every practice, which the NCAA couldn't do. Matt agreed that it was a dumb rule. He thought the NCAA should just give a set number of people that were allowed to be around the basketball program in any capacity and not worry so much about job titles.

Matt also understood that the NCAA didn't make the rules. The general public didn't know that. Many, heck maybe even most, basketball and football coaches didn't know that.

The rules were made when a school or conference proposed new legislation. Then each school that is a member of the NCAA casts a vote. The schools decide what new rules to adopt and which ones to get rid of. The NCAA itself didn't propose legislation, at least they hadn't in the past. Under the new NCAA president, things were changing and the NCAA staff itself was starting to try to influence things more than they had in the past.

Matt listened as Lisa explained all of this to Culp. This was a trap that most NCAA investigators fell into. Matt, himself, had gone through this routine several times before he realized it did no good. The coaches didn't want to listen to an explanation or even understand how NCAA rules were made. They only wanted to coach and worry about their own team then complain whenever they had a chance. ESPN and Dick Vitale echoed the coaches' complaints on air without trying to understand the process which emboldened the coaches to complain even further.

Lisa finally got back on track with her next question. "So you both were at Southwest Metro State right in the middle of the recruiting scandal they went through? Didn't they have to forfeit an entire season and didn't their head coach get a show cause, which basically banned him from coaching for three years?"

Again Culp grinned before answering. "Actually I left right before that investigation began. I took a job at another school, but I was interviewed by one of your people for the case."

Lisa hadn't known that. She would have to go back and dig through that case and read through Culp's interview to learn more about him and see if he contradicted himself now.

"So you weren't punished and neither was Ken Reid?" Lisa asked.

"Punished?" Culp retorted. "For what? We did nothing wrong. There was a kid on that team that didn't get to play as much as his mom wanted so they made up some things that brought down a great coach."

Lisa started to respond, but Matt interrupted. "I think you two can talk about the old days after we're done, but let's move on for now with this issue."

Matt could tell that Lisa didn't like being interrupted, but she did steer things back on track.

"Okay, so you and Reid worked together for a while. Did you stay in touch with each other over the years?"

"Sure, I stay in touch with everyone in the coaching world. When I heard that Reid had taken a job at a junior college I congratulated him and told him that if he ever had any good players he should let me know. Once I got to GCSU I regularly contacted Reid to talk about JC players he had seen."

Lisa considered this a moment, then asked, "so were you the one that approached him about the job opening at GCSU?"

Culp grinned his evil little grin then responded. "Now you know as well as I do that an assistant coach doesn't make the decision about who to hire on staff. I mentioned to Coach McEnroe that Reid was a good coach and a good recruiter. I told him he should take a long look at adding him to our staff, but I didn't make the decision to hire him. Only the head coach makes those decisions."

"But Coach McEnroe trusted you and didn't look that hard at anyone else did he?" Lisa asked.

"If you say so," was all Culp answered.

"Did you know about the two good players that were playing for Reid at the time?"

Again, the little grin appeared as Culp answered. "What kind of recruiter would I be if I didn't know about those two? You must not think I'm very good at my job if you ask that type of question. Of course I knew about them! I know about every good player in our area that might possibly come here. I know you might be enthralled with my good looks and charm, but I actually know about the business of basketball."

Matt could tell that Culp was really getting to Lisa. She clinched her jaw and sat up a little straighter each time Culp got in a little dig. Matt might find an opportunity to mention it to her, but then again he might not. He didn't think she would take it well if he did say something about it to her.

Lisa forged ahead. "So if you knew about the players, is that why you recommended Reid to Coach McEnroe?"

"It certainly didn't hurt! But Ken Reid was my friend and a pretty good coach. I would have recommended him even if he didn't have those players. It was an added bonus that he had two guys that played positions where we had a need."

Matt could tell that Lisa was frustrated. These types of cases were often frustrating because it is difficult to prove that someone got hired only on the basis of them being able to bring good players with them. Unless there was something in writing or a coach just flat out admitted it, the investigation was often left with things that looked bad, but had no proof. Under the law absence of proof wouldn't fly, but in the NCAA world one might make a case built on circumstantial evidence, but it would be very difficult.

Matt had worked on a couple of these types of cases before. Lisa didn't have any experience with this, but she was determined to move forward.

"So Mr. Culp," Lisa began. "Did you ever tell Ken Reid that part of the deal of him being hired was if he could deliver those two players?"

"Whoa, Mr. Culp is it now?" Culp snorted. "Suddenly we are very formal! Does that indicate that you have come to the serious part of the interview?"

Matt had to laugh inwardly. Culp was a real piece of work. He seemed to be enjoying needling Lisa, but Matt didn't know why. It could be that she was from the NCAA and Culp might just not look too favorably on that organization. Or it could be that Culp liked to hassle women. Matt couldn't tell for sure, but he could understand why the AD called Culp "smarmy".

Culp continued, "I never told Ken that if he delivered the players he would be hired. It was understood by all that those two players were really important to us, but I never said those words. The fact is that I didn't hire Ken Reid, Coach McEnroe did. Would Coach McEnroe have hired Ken Reid if he didn't bring those players with him? I guess only he can answer that question. I knew that the two players were important to us and Ken knew that he better deliver those players."

Lisa looked over at Matt. Matt could tell she was trying to figure out what to do next. She had an idea of what had happened, but nobody came right out and said that Ken Reid would only be hired if two players came with him, which would have wrapped this all up nice and tidy.

The NCAA had been dealing with this type of issue for years. Danny Manning was often cited as the example when talking about this issue. In the mid 1980's Danny Manning was an outstanding basketball player in

Greensboro, North Carolina and was widely regarded as the number one high school recruit his senior year. Both North Carolina and North Carolina State battled during the recruitment of Manning. A few days before Manning was going to announce where he would attend college and play basketball, Ed Manning, Danny's father, was hired as an assistant basketball coach at Kansas. At the time, the elder Manning was allegedly driving an 18-wheel truck and hadn't coached basketball for years.

Of course, Danny chose to play at Kansas with his father coaching him and ended up winning a national championship. When Danny Manning made his decision he said he had chosen Kansas to be closer to his parents. Larry Brown, the coach of Kansas at the time, said it wasn't a package deal, but he knew people would view it that way. NCAA rules prevent colleges from giving benefits to a prospect or the family of a prospect. One would argue that a high paying job as an assistant basketball coach could be considered a benefit, especially if the person who obtained that job had not been coaching for years.

Even with all of that, it was still extremely difficult to prove that Manning's father only got the job because his son was the top recruit that year. The father had played college basketball and at one time had coached. Everybody believed the job was given to secure Danny Manning's commitment, but what proof was there?

This was a similar issue. Ken Reid was coaching junior college basketball so he was a viable candidate. The NCAA was trying to show that Reid only got the job because his two players would come with him and that would be a benefit for the two players. Matt knew they would have to speak with Reid and the two players.

The interview with Culp concluded. Lisa couldn't get him out of the room fast enough. Culp snickered as he stood up and shook hands. He left the room with the same grin on his face that he had when answering questions.

Lisa didn't want to show any signs of not being in total control. The truth was that Culp had gotten to her a little, but she would never admit that. She didn't like him and was going to do her best to bring him down.

"What's your next move?" Matt asked.

"I think I'm going to go back to headquarters and discuss this with my supervisor. I'll be in touch with you after we decide where to go from here." Lisa answered.

They shook hands and Lisa gathered up her belongings. Shawn walked her out to her car. Matt met with the AD to update him on where things stood. They agreed to wait for the NCAA to make the next move. Matt wasn't going to just wait though. He was going to gather as much background information as he could. The NCAA loved to threaten schools with tampering if they even hinted at doing anything without the NCAA first giving its blessing, but Matt was seasoned enough to know that he could start preparing a few things. Working with the NCAA was always interesting. Lisa seemed okay, but she definitely had a chip on her shoulder. Matt knew she wanted to show how good she was. Matt had worked with many of the NCAA enforcement staff so this was nothing new to him. Time to began digging!

CHAPTER FOUR

Lisa met the following morning with her supervisor back at the NCAA national office in Indianapolis. Her official title was assistant director of enforcement. Her supervisor was one of the six directors of enforcement. In the early 90's the enforcement staff had 14 investigators divided up into four teams. Each team had a director of enforcement that supervised his or her group of three to four investigators.

Over the next decade, the enforcement staff grew tremendously. There were now around 40 investigators divided up into several teams. There was a basketball focus group that was formed to look at the culture of summer basketball, AAU teams and the outside influences involved in the basketball world of young recruits. An Agents, Gambling and Amateurism group was formed followed by a football focus group.

Each group worked to establish and make a name for itself. This resulted in a culture of competition within the enforcement staff. Each group competed to be the next to bring down a school, gain notoriety and more resources for its group. This was the dirty little secret that the powers that be in enforcement didn't realize was occurring, but that the people on the outside observed. The supervision of this competition was lax at best so many of the groups had developed very poor reputations amongst the universities and colleges that make up the NCAA.

Very few people outside of the NCAA enforcement staff tried to explain to the powers that be how this culture was hurting the reputation of the enforcement staff as a whole. Those who did try were met with stoic faces and a refusal to consider that maybe there were problems within the enforcement staff itself.

Lisa's supervisor, Ed Raines, was a long time enforcement staff employee who had been through the old days, seen the growth, heard rumors of problems and wanted to address them, but was ill equipped to do so. He had never worked at a university so he wasn't able to understand how outsiders from the respective universities saw things, no matter how hard he tried. Ed had a reputation of being a "good guy", but a dyed-in-the-wool NCAA die-hard. Ed couldn't see the problems within the enforcement staff because he was too close to the situation and only had one perspective.

Lisa sat down with Ed to begin explaining what her initial look at GCSU had uncovered. "I believe that they hired Ken Reid conditioned upon him bringing the two JC players with him, but nobody came right out and said that. It is going to be hard to prove."

Ed thought this over for a moment. "These are some of the toughest cases to prove, but we do have the burden of proof, well not outright proof, but a preponderance of the evidence is required. Do you think you can get there?"

Lisa weighed that question in her mind. She wanted so desperately to win a case like this. That would really set her apart from the other enforcement staff members. It would be difficult, but she had to give it her best.

"I'm not sure if we will ever get there, but I have a few ideas in mind. I'd like to give it a try."

"Well we owe it to the membership," Ed replied. Ed said things like this a lot and he truly believed it.

"Tell me something Ed," Lisa began. "GCSU hired Matt Colter to represent them in this investigation. Didn't Matt work here in the past?"

Ed laughed a bit and said "he sure did. He worked for me. I was his supervisor. He was one of the quickest learners we ever had. He was only here a short time, but he presented a number of cases in front of the Committee on Infractions in his short time. He had a talent for getting coaches and student-athletes to talk to him. They would just open up with him. I've never seen anything like it before or since."

"Is he going to be difficult for me to deal with?" Lisa asked.

"No, I don't think so. He is very honest and still appreciates the difficulty we face in trying to uncover information. He visits us every so often just to stay in touch and always expresses his admiration for the tough jobs we have. I'm surprised you have never met him during one of his visits."

Lisa wasn't so sure about Matt Colter's admiration, but she could sense that Ed was fond of Matt so she didn't press it. She would be careful dealing with him and definitely wouldn't trust him.

"If you have any problems with Matt, let me know and I'll run interference for you, but I doubt you'll have any problems. In fact, you should watch him and try to learn from him if you can."

That was the last thing Lisa was going to do! Learn from Matt Colter? She didn't trust him any further than she could throw him!

Matt followed up the interviews by first meeting with the AD to let him know how things went. Matt then walked over to the President's office. Matt had learned over the years that while he would keep the AD informed, he reported to the president of the school and kept some information solely for the president's ears. Matt sat down in President Scott's office.

"Matt I only have a few moments before I have a faculty meeting so let's make this quick. How did things go?" President Scott got right to the point.

"I just wanted to update you and ask a couple of questions." Matt gave a quick recap of the interviews then asked "what is the university's thinking regarding Coach McEnroe? Do you want to protect him?"

President Scott leaned back in his chair. "This is all protected under attorney/client privilege, right?"

"Absolutely, everything you tell me will remain with me," Matt confirmed.

"Let's just say we'd like to figure out a way to have Coach McEnroe leave the university without bringing our reputation down or having it cost us a boatload of money. I was hesitant when we hired him and he has confirmed my worst fears. He doesn't care about education, isn't engaged in his own team's recruiting, has hired a couple of thugs in the role of assistant coaches. They aren't good representatives of our university. We can fire him for cause so we'd like to find a reason to get rid of him, but we don't want the negative things that come with a major NCAA infraction. In a perfect world, we would find just enough to justify firing him without paying the remaining years on his contract, but not enough to besmirch the reputation of the university."

Matt had suspected as much. He got definite vibes that the university and Coach McEnroe were on different pages. The university hired Matt and employed him, but he would not make up things to help them get rid of an employee.

Matt had experience as a player as well as having worked in enforcement at the NCAA. As a college senior Matt had lead his team to the elite eight of the NCAA basketball tournament. His school was not one of the power schools so the fact that they won a game was noteworthy. When they won their second game to make it to the sweet sixteen they started getting national attention. In the sweet sixteen game, Matt had scored 28 points, dished off 14 assists, pulled down 11 rebounds and blocked 9 shots, narrowly missing a quadruple double. His team had upset one of the favorites to win the championship so his Cinderella story became a national story.

That had catapulted Matt into receiving invitations to various NBA team tryouts. He had performed well there and at the Portsmouth Invitational in front of NBA scouts. Matt had been drafted in the second round and played three seasons in the NBA before being released.

Matt had played very good defense, could shoot threes with the best of them and was a good passer. His main problem was that he couldn't take the ball to the hole and people started realizing that. When defenders crowded him, Matt didn't have the skills to drive past them. Matt saw the writing on the wall, but it was a testimony to his basketball intelligence that he was able to last three years in the NBA making a nice salary.

Knowing that his NBA career wouldn't be a long one, Matt enrolled in law school and took courses whenever his schedule permitted. He worked out a deal with the law school dean, who happened to be a big professional basketball fan. The dean constructed a favorable schedule for Matt to take classes during his breaks from basketball. It was a feather in the cap of the law school to have an NBA player enrolled and they milked as much publicity out of it as they could. Matt didn't mind because it was a win-win situation for everyone.

Matt then went and played in Europe for three more years making a very nice salary and taking law school classes during his breaks. He was only 28 years old and had a great future ahead of him. Everything changed in an instant one day while he was playing in Greece. He stumbled upon something that changed his life.

Matt was out shopping on one of his off days when he observed the teen-aged daughter of his team owner. The owner was a very wealthy member of the Greek community. Matt had seen the owner's children out before, but always accompanied by bodyguards.

On this occasion, the daughter was out with friends and Matt didn't see a bodyguard anywhere. Looking more closely, Matt noticed a couple of men following the girl and at first, thought they must be bodyguards keeping a distance to give the girls a sense of freedom. Upon inspecting more closely, Matt realized the two men were up to no good. He sprinted towards the girls just as one of the men made a grab for the daughter. Matt knocked him flying which attracted a local policeman. When the men saw the police they took off only to be caught later.

The story made national news. The men confessed that they were going to kidnap the girl and hold her for ransom. The owner of the team thanked Matt profusely. Unfortunately for Matt, he tore up his knee when he plowed into the kidnapper. Matt's playing days were over. The owner was so grateful that he gave Matt a reward of five million dollars. Matt tried to turn down the reward, but the owner would not hear of it.

Matt returned to the US. He had enough money to satisfy his desires, but what now? Matt lived well, invested wisely and was financially very well off. Soon, he grew tired of living a life of leisure so he finished law school, took the bar exam and was hired by the NCAA upon graduation. After working at the NCAA for a couple of years, he had become frustrated being at the NCAA and some of the things he saw as hypocritical.

Matt didn't have to work so he resigned from the NCAA. Two weeks after retiring from the NCAA, the parents of a college football player who thought their son had received bad treatment from a coach contacted Matt. Matt found out that the parents were friends of one of the NCAA enforcement staff members. That person had given them Matt's name. Matt worked with the family and the school to resolve the problem without a lawsuit. During that experience, Matt discovered that he enjoyed helping kids so he began representing student-athletes. A few schools noticed his work and hired him to represent them in NCAA matters.

Matt was fortunate in that he could say no to any job. If he didn't like the people, didn't feel they were being honest, he could say no at any time. This gave him the freedom to do what he wanted. He didn't need the money so there was no pressure to compromise his standards. He explained that at the outset of each case. Matt gained a reputation quickly. There were only four or five firms that regularly represented colleges and universities in NCAA enforcement matters.

Mike Glazier and his group at Bond, Schoeneck & King were well known. Chuck Smrt at the Compliance Group, Mark Jones at Ice Miller and a relative new group at Lightfoot, Franklin and White were the only other firms who routinely represented the schools. There were many other so called "experts" who liked to see their names in the paper and for some reason the newspapers used them, but they were less "experts" and more self-promoters. Matt didn't feel like a competitor because he didn't actively seek business. He took cases that interested him or where he had friends involved in some way.

Matt was representing GCSU as a favor to a friend in the athletics office. Matt didn't particularly care for the AD, Mike Love, but he did appreciate President Scott's direct manner. Matt would represent guilty clients if they wanted to do the right thing. If they just wanted to get away with cheating, he had the luxury of saying no and walking away.

Matt didn't buy into the prevailing theory that he had to provide everyone a good defense. He did believe everyone deserved a good defense, but didn't believe he had to be the one who provided that defense. He thought more along the lines that everyone deserved a second chance as long as they took the appropriate steps to right their wrong and changed. He found comfort in the knowledge that he could walk away at any time from the business and still live a good life. That set him apart from everyone else.

Matt could tell that GCSU's coaches had hired Reid because he had the two good players. He didn't think the NCAA would be able to prove that because the only two people who knew were Coach McEnroe and Rancy Culp and neither of them confessed.

Matt had a few ideas in the GCSU matter, but thought he better check in with Lisa at the NCAA first. The NCAA was very territorial and didn't like anyone moving forward without getting its approval first. He dialed Lisa's number. She picked up after the first ring.

"Hello, Lisa Lasham speaking."

"Hi Lisa, this is Matt Colter. I'm wondering if you've had time to figure out the next steps."

"Mr. Colter," Lisa began.

"Please, call me Matt."

"Mr. Colter, I just spoke with my supervisor and haven't really had time to outline the next steps in the investigation."

Matt smiled picturing how upset Lisa seemed to be just because of a phone call. He didn't know why, but he enjoyed tweaking some of the young, uptight NCAA enforcement staff members. He knew they were just trying to do their job and get noticed, but he was always amazed at how quickly they began treating him like the enemy. If one of them ever just talked with him like a normal person he would go out of his way to help them in any way he could without compromising his client.

"Lisa, I hope you don't mind if I call you Lisa, do you want to know what I would do?"

"Not particularly, but go ahead and tell me because I know you will."

Matt laughed to himself. "I would track down the two players and see what they have to say. They will probably protect their coach, but they might slip up and let us get a little better understanding regarding what was going on at that time."

"Are you trying to help me uncover problems? Doesn't that fly in the face of your duty to protect your client?"

"Ah, you see, that is where you are mistaken," Matt explained. "GCSU wants to be completely honest and straight forward. If there were problems, they want to uncover and fix them. They have instructed me to get to the bottom of this and they will let the chips fall where they may."

"Well that is a refreshing approach, but pardon me if I don't buy everything that you are selling," Lisa responded.

"So, are you going to contact the players?" Matt asked.

"I'll think it over and get back in touch with you."

"Great, that is all I can ask," Matt stated. "Nice talking with you and tell Ed hi for me."

"How did you know that I reported to Ed?"

"Oh, I know a lot of things about the NCAA enforcement staff. It isn't a big secret is it?"

Lisa was infuriated with Matt's attitude. She could tell he was thoroughly enjoying himself. She had to find a way to stop him from getting under her skin.

"I'll be in touch, Mr. Colter", Lisa said emphasizing the Mister. With that she hung up. Matt laughed and hung up his phone. He would start trying to track down the players to learn what he could about them. He had to be careful not to step on Lisa's toes. The NCAA didn't like it when a school tried to get out ahead of them which wasn't a hard thing to do. Lisa was probably working three or four cases right now and this was Matt's only one. Matt had to work hard to keep things on the slow pace at which the enforcement staff worked.

CHAPTER FIVE

The following morning Matt assembled his team. Since he was self-employed and didn't have to work, he had never hired an office staff. That didn't mean that he didn't have help though. In the middle of a prior investigation, Matt had stumbled upon Holly Cash. Holly was drop dead gorgeous, standing five foot seven inches, with beautiful full auburn hair. She obviously worked out because one glance at her revealed a body that was fit and strong.

Matt had tried to get close to Holly during the investigation, but she had thwarted every attempt he had made to get to know her better. Matt finally drew upon his courage and asked Holly out, but she told him that she was happily married.

After getting over his embarrassment, Matt found that he liked Holly's personality and wanted to be friends with her. Matt apologized to Holly saying he would have never asked her out if he knew she was married. He explained that he believed in marriage, in fact he wanted to get married himself some day.

They struck up a friendship during the course of the investigation. Matt found out that Holly was a computer hacker with unbelievable skills. Holly had been able to get some information that Matt would have never been able to find. She wouldn't reveal her secrets, but told Matt she would help if it was for a good cause.

Matt found out that Holly's husband had invented some computer program that made him incredibly wealthy. Holly had introduced Matt to her husband and they had become friends as well. Matt and Holly were in similar situations. Matt worked because he liked it, but didn't represent people he didn't like. Holly worked as a consultant whenever she wanted, but didn't need the money.

As their friendship grew and Holly came to know Matt better she liked how he worked and the types of clients he represented. Holly told Matt that she would be happy to do some work for him if he ever had use of her computer skills. Matt told her that he probably couldn't afford her. Holly had laughed and said she never worked for money. She donated whatever she was paid to a cancer research group.

Matt had hired Holly on his very next case and her help had proven invaluable. He continued to employ her whenever he had need and they had become very good friends. Holly, good to her word, had donated whatever Matt paid her to the cancer research group, dedicated to finding a cure for cancer. Matt found out that Holly had lost both of her parents to cancer.

The other person that joined the group was Cedric Booker. You couldn't ignore Booker if he walked into a room. Booker towered over everyone at six foot eight, was African-American, had a shiny bald head, but if that wasn't intimidating enough, Booker had muscles that stretched the fabric of everything he wore. His muscles had muscles. Booker also dressed very well which Matt couldn't believe since it had to be difficult to find clothing in his size.

Matt had met Cedric when they had been on the same NBA team. Cedric had been called the enforcer when he played. Nobody messed with him. Cedric hadn't been that great of a player, but was a ferocious rebounder. When Matt had been released, Ced was the first one to reach out to him. Ced had been playing in Europe and told Matt that he would do well there. Ced had put Matt in touch with the right people and they found themselves on the same team.

A strong friendship had developed between them. After Matt's injury he had stayed in touch with Ced. When Ced retired, he had visited Matt, learned about Matt's investment strategies, then studied the market. It turned out that Ced had an aptitude for investing and he had done very very well. Matt suggested that Ced find employment with a venture capitol firm, but Ced told Matt he would be bored to death doing something like that.

Matt had needed some muscle on one of his cases and asked Ced to join him during a search for an informant. That search had led them to a seedy part of town, they had run into some trouble. Trouble meaning they were jumped by four guys, but Ced had proven to be more than a match for their assailants. Matt had barely broken a sweat in the battle, while Ced had incapacitated all four of the attackers.

Ced told Matt that he enjoyed the excitement and was available whenever Matt needed him. Matt used Ced on every case since then, sometimes just as a resource to bounce ideas and thoughts off of, at other times as an active member of his team.

That was Matt's team. A beautiful auburn-haired hacker and a big muscle-bound former basketball player, both working more for fun than for money. Whenever Matt went somewhere with Holly and Ced he laughed at the heads that turned their way. He was never sure who drew more attention, Holly or Ced.

So Matt had no full-time employees. He would get them together whenever he took on a case and tell them what it was about. He might have need of them or might not, but wanted them to be informed from the beginning. This time Matt already had a need for Holly as he explained the case to them.

"Holly, what I'm going to need is to find the two former players who played for Ken Reid at the North Dakota junior college and then followed him to GCSU. Here is the media guide from GCSU so you can get their information. The two players names are Tyron Washington and Len Mallard. See if you can track down where they are now and get an address, phone number, cell phone, email, the usual."

"Okay I'll get on it. When do you need it?"

"By the end of the week," Matt replied. "Is that okay?"

Holly laughed. "Oh Matt, sweet Matt, you really aren't a computer guy are you? I'll have something in a couple of hours. Let's meet tomorrow morning and I'll have everything written up for you. It should be no problem finding these guys."

"Do you have anything for me to do?" Ced asked.

"Not yet, but depending upon what Holly finds, I may need you to physically track down these guys so we can interview them. I'll get back to you. Want to go to the gym with me right now?"

"So you can see how a real man works out?" With that Ced gave a big laugh and headed for the door. "Sure, let's go. You never know when you might need your own muscles."

Matt grabbed his workout gear and followed Ced out the door. The truth of the matter was that Matt was in incredible shape. He had washboard abs, a thick chest and arms, but standing next to Ced made Matt look like a little boy. Matt knew that, but was comfortable enough to not let it bother him.

Good as her word, the following morning Holly greeted Matt and handed him a manila folder. "I'll give you the short version," Holly began. "Tyron Washington is playing professional basketball in Turkey. He has a cell phone, but it only works sporadically. He is doing pretty well and making good money, which he saves. He sends a large amount home to his mother each month."

"Did you happen to get his mother's contact information?"

"Matt, I'm hurt that you would even ask such a question. I'm nothing if not thorough. You have her address, phone number and e-mail," Holly replied.

"Great, you don't happen to know if she'll talk to me do you?" Matt joked.

"No, but if you want me to find out I can go through her email and Facebook pages to see how open she is to communicating with strangers."

Matt laughed and told Holly that wouldn't be necessary. "I know that Ced is anxious to get involved so I'll have him do it the old-fashioned way. He can physically contact her and see if she'll speak with us. What did you find out about the other guy?"

Holly looked serious as she responded. "Len Mallard went off the deep end. He never graduated from GCSU. He auditioned for a couple of NBA teams, but didn't do well. He went overseas to play, but didn't do well there either. He came back home and got a couple of menial jobs, but didn't last long at either one."

"That's a shame," Matt answered. "I saw that happen with so many guys who thought they would be playing professional basketball. There are only a small number of open jobs in the NBA each year and thousands of people who want to fill them. Even really good players find out they aren't good enough."

"Yes, well Len Mallard wasn't good enough," Holly stated. "After being fired from his last job he just completely disappeared. He has no banking history, doesn't pay bills or email anyone. He has completely fallen off the grid. The last history I have of him is from about six weeks ago when he was cited for drunk and disorderly conduct. He spent a night in jail then was released. From that moment on there is no electronic trail."

Matt thought that over for a few moments. He always felt some sadness when he heard of athletes failing to grasp how valuable a college education was. They banked on becoming a professional athlete and didn't develop the skills necessary to succeed outside of athletics and didn't take advantage of the education they had been provided.

"Holly, how common is it for someone to just disappear off the grid like that?"

"I don't believe it is as uncommon as you might think. The reason we don't see if that often is because the people we usually are involved with are college educated. They have jobs and families. In Len Mallard's case, I think it is one of two things. He is either homeless living on the streets or he is dead."

"That sounds like it is right up Ced's alley. I guess I'll track down Tyron Washington's mother and leave Len Mallard up to Ced."

"Well it is all there in my report. You have everything I could find."

Matt thanked Holly and told her he would donate what he would have paid her to the cancer research group she supported. Holly thanked Matt and wished him good luck. "Let me know what you find out about Len Mallard. Learning what happened to him will help me figure out if there is something I'm missing when I'm searching for someone electronically."

Holly got up and walked to the door. Matt followed behind and thanked her again. He closed the door as she exited. He thought he would start trying to track down the mothers of both players to see if he could locate them. Then he would see what the NCAA wanted to do. He didn't think Lisa Lasham would be able to locate either player, but didn't want to overstep his bounds before she told him that she had given up.

CHAPTER SIX

Ced Booker loved being in Los Angeles. He loved the sunshine, the beaches nearby and the people. Ced didn't even mind the stares he got in L.A. He was used to the stares, but the fresh air and sunshine made it less annoying there.

Matt had explained to Ced what Holly had been able and unable to find regarding Len Mallard. Matt had asked Ced to go to Los Angeles to track down Mallard's mother.

Ced rented a convertible so he could enjoy the sunshine. Driving down the 405 freeway with the wind swirling around him was Ced's idea of fun. He knew that other motorists stared at him as he drove by, but that just made it even more fun.

According to the information in Holly's report, Len Mallard's mother lived in Long Beach. Mallard had attended Poly High School then received a scholarship from USC. Unfortunately, he had not been admitted due to some very bad grades so he had gone to a junior college in North Dakota. Ced was confused about how Mallard had gone from Southern California to North Dakota. There were a number of good junior colleges in Southern California. Many that played pretty good basketball, so why had he gone to North Dakota?

Ced had little trouble finding the last known address for Mallard. Ced had contacts all over the United States and he had called one of them before coming to California. He maneuvered through the streets ending up on Umatella Ave. He pulled over to the curb, parked the car and disengaged his large frame from the front seat. Standing at full height, Ced stretched to emphasize his physique even more. He knew he was being watched and wanted to send a message saying don't mess with me. His contact, Reggie Maxwell, came out of the building.

"What's up my large brother?" Maxwell boomed as he walked towards Ced.

"How's it going Reggie?" Ced replied.

Ced had met Reggie when Ced was playing in the NBA. He couldn't recall who had introduced them, but Reggie was always around when Ced played against the Lakers or Clippers. Ced had gone out with a group of people after one of the games. The group included Reggie and some of his "associates". Ced wasn't really sure what Reggie did to earn his money, but Ced knew that Reggie could help him navigate through any difficulties he might encounter in Southern California.

Ced had told Reggie over the phone that he was trying to find Len Mallard or Mallard's mother. Reggie greeted Ced with a quick shake of hands then got right to the point.

"Look, I don't want to sit out here and talk to you for a long time. You draw too much attention, which shocks me because of your small quiet demeanor! Here is the work address for Len Mallard's mama. She goes by the name of Shirly Jo and you don't want to mess with her!"

"Any idea how I can find Len Mallard himself?" Ced asked.

"Last I heard, Mallard was living under a bridge down by the aquarium. He got involved in selling drugs and his mother found out so she kicked him out of her home. "

"That is some real tough love! Thanks Reggie. I owe you"

"Yes, you do and don't worry, I'll collect sometime!"

"Don't' forget how many times I hooked you up with tickets back in the day," Ced reminded him.

"That's right, you did. I guess I still owe you then. Consider this a little bit of the payment!" With that the two said goodbye and Ced got back into his car. He headed for Shirly Jo Mallard's work address.

Shirly Jo worked at a health clinic. Ced punched the address into his GPS then followed the directions. He pulled into the parking lot, exited the car then walked inside. There were about ten people waiting in the front room. Ced wandered over to the desk.

Sitting behind the desk was a 20 something young woman. Not bad looking Ced thought to himself. He smiled as he approached her. She looked up at him and smiled.

"Hello sir, what can we do for you today?" she asked very cheerfully.

"Well pretty lady, first of all you can stop calling me sir. I'm working undercover and don't want people to know I'm a knight!"

The girl laughed then said, "that is a new one and don't you think calling me pretty lady is a little sexist?"

Ced leaned down on the desk. "It isn't sexist if it is true."

She laughed again. "Why don't you tell me why you are here. You don't look like our typical clinic patients."

Ced decided on the spot to be direct with her because it appeared she didn't put up with any bull.

"I'm trying to locate Shirly Jo Mallard. I need to discuss something with her."

"Is it about her son? Did something happen to him?"

"What do you know about her son?" Ced asked.

"I know that Shirly Jo had to make some tough decisions about him. She told him she would always love and support him, but that he couldn't stay with her if he wasn't going to find a job and get cleaned up."

"So he uses drugs as well as sells them?"

Suddenly the young woman looked alarmed. She realized that others were listening. "I don't think it is my place to talk about this. I'm, no we all, are pretty protective of Shirly Jo. Everyone loves her. Let me go see if she is available."

The young woman went into the back. Ced turned around to find everyone in the room staring at him. He stared right back and they all lowered their heads.

The woman came back to the desk. "Come right this way sir, uh Mr? You never did tell me your name."

"No I didn't, maybe I could do that over dinner tonight."

She laughed again and said "I don't think I could handle someone like you."

"Don't sell yourself short. I think you do just fine. And I'm Ced by the way, Ced Booker, pleased to meet you!"

She smiled again then lead him to the back.

"Shirly is in room 2 waiting for you. Be nice to her and then we'll see about dinner!" She laughed again and walked away.

Too bad she is so young, Ced thought as he watched her walk away. That is the type of girl I could seriously fall for, brains and beauty. He turned back around and walked to a door that was marked with a big "2" on it. He knocked lightly before opening the door.

Shirly Jo was seated waiting for him. She looked determined.

"Tell me straight away if something has happened to my son. Don't beat around the bush, I want to know!"

Ced was taken back by the force of her personality. He could tell she was strong because it took something very strong to make him take notice. The room seemed very small with the two of them in it.

"I don't have any information about your son. I'm trying to find him so I can ask him about what happened with his basketball coach."

"Are you from the police?" Shirly Jo asked.

"No ma'am. I work with an attorney who is representing GCSU. The NCAA is looking into the basketball program at GCSU."

"And y'all are defending them?"

"The person I work for is trying to help them figure out what happened. GCSU is paying him, but he just wants to get to the truth."

"Yeah, sure I've heard that before," Shirly Jo snorted. "I've heard a lot of things when it comes to my son. None of those people wanted to help him. They only cared about themselves."

Ced pulled a chair over and sat down. He wasn't sure where to begin so he thought he'd let her tell him the whole story.

"Ma'am, if you will, I'd like to hear the whole story. How did your son get to North Dakota then move on to GCSU. What happened?"

"How much time you got?" Shirly Jo asked.

"As much time as you need," Ced responded. "I'm sorry to come to your work. Would you rather wait until after you are done working?"

"It is going to take more than a few minutes. I get off in 45 minutes. Can you wait until then?"

"Sure, no problem. I'll go sit out in my car and when you come out we can decide where you want to talk."

Shirly Jo looked at Ced. "You are one big man, but I can tell you have a good heart."

"You are very perceptive," Ced smiled. "I'll be completely honest with you. I usually have a long story and know all about what happened before I come talk to someone. In this instance I don't have any idea what really happened so I'm completely open to hearing what you have to say."

"Oh, I'll tell you. I'm mad about it, but there isn't much anyone can do."

"I'll wait outside then we can see if that is true."

Ced stood up and walked to the door. "Ma'am, I can't promise you anything, but if someone did something wrong to your son, we'll figure out how to make them pay."

The look on Shirly Jo's face told Ced he had hit home with that remark. He left the room, passing the front desk as he walked. He smiled at the young woman and told her he would call her later for that dinner. She smiled at him as he walked out the front.

Thirty minutes later Shirly Jo came out the same door. Ced saw her and got out of his car. "I thought you said you got off in 45 minutes?"

"I did, but you caused quite a stir with our receptionist. She told the doctor and when he found out I was meeting you he let me go early."

"Where do you want to talk?" Ced asked.

"I was going to walk to the bus stop, but if you'll drive we can go to my home and talk."

Ced agreed and they quickly drove about ten minutes to a small older home.

"This is a nice little place you have," Ced remarked. "Have you lived here long?"

Shirly Jo walked up the front steps and used her keys to open the door.

"My father purchased this house in 1956 after he got out of the military. I've lived here all my life. I had one brother, but he was killed in high school. When my father passed, I was the only child so he left me this house."

Ced could tell it was a modest home, but that Shirly Jo kept it clean. There were photos of children along the wall. Shirly Jo noticed Ced looking at photos.

"Those are my babies. I have three children. Len is the oldest, then my daughter Grace is a senior in high school and Dwayne is the baby. He is in 10th grade. And before you ask, no there is no man in my life. I've done a bad job picking men. Len's father was my high school boyfriend. He ran away as fast as he could after finding out I was pregnant. I married a good man a few years later and we had the other two kids. My husband died of a heart attack at work. He was 34. Then I tried one more time and met a man I thought I would live the rest of my life with. I caught him fooling around with one of my friends. I swore off men after that and decided to raise my babies alone."

"So tell me about Len. I know he played at Poly then signed with USC. What happened after that?"

Shirly Jo stared out the window. Ced could tell the memories brought pain.

"Len wasn't a bad boy. He just needed a man in his life. I've seen plenty of men I wouldn't want my daughter to be involved with. Men who don't know what it means to be a good father or husband. They just want to play around moving from one woman to the next. No respect for women. So it is that much harder to realize I raised one of those men myself. We complain about men, but a lot of the blame falls on absentee parents. I wasn't there enough for Len. I know I had to work and it couldn't be helped, but I still am to blame."

Ced was going to ask another question, but realized Shirly Jo needed to talk so he let her go on.

"When Len got to high school I knew he was a ladies man. I didn't like it and I told him many times. He loved me, but treated those girls horribly. I just prayed he would get a scholarship and grow up in college. When USC offered him a scholarship I thought it was the answer to my prayers, but then Len's grades weren't good enough. The coaches tried, but they finally dropped Len.

"About that time he was involved with two or three different girls. For all I know it might have been six or seven. Two of the girls found out about each other and they both had older brothers. The brothers of both girls threatened Len and were planning on doing him some harm. Len was afraid so I called my cousin who lives in North Dakota. She works at a junior college. I told her about Len, about not getting admitted at USC and the trouble he was in. She told me she knew the basketball coach at her school and would talk to him. The next morning I received a phone call from the coach who told me he would love to have Len on his team and could arrange for some financial help."

"I told Len about it and he jumped at the chance to get out of Dodge so to speak. Looking back I should have spent more time finding out a little bit about that coach. Coach Reid is a bad, corrupt man."

Ced waited for a pause then asked, "you said Coach Reid could arrange for some financial help, do you know what that was?"

Shirly Jo shook her head. "No, I never really heard from Len about it. He said he was on scholarship, but I don't think junior colleges give out many scholarships do they?"

Before Ced could respond she continued.

"Anyway, Len told me he had a job on campus, but I have no idea what he did. He didn't like North Dakota, but was afraid to come back here. I told him to stick it out, work hard and if he got the grades maybe he could come play for USC."

"So what happened?" Ced asked.

"Len did okay. He got Bs and Cs in school. He did very well in basketball. After two years he was getting a lot of offers from big schools. Then one day he said he was going to GCSU. I didn't understand it. GCSU had never been mentioned as a possibility then suddenly overnight Len wants to go there? It made no sense."

"But didn't Coach Reid go there? Maybe that is why Len decided to go there so he could stay with his coach?" Ced suggested.

Shirly Jo laughed. "Len hated Coach Reid. He always told me he couldn't wait to get away from him. That is what really makes no sense. Len constantly complained about how Coach Reid treated him and the team. I don't know what that man did, but he made my son go to GCSU."

Ced thought about that. If this was all true, what did Ken Reid have that made Len follow him to GCSU, especially if Len really did hate him?

"Did you ever ask Len why he chose GCSU?"

Shirly Jo was staring out the window again, but looked straight at Ced when she answered.

"Of course I asked him. He said 'mama you wouldn't understand. I had to go with him.' I could never get him to tell me why. He was a grown man at that point, but I knew Coach Reid had done something wrong. He was bad for my son and it turned out that he didn't care about him at all. He used Len to get a better paying job for himself then discarded Len like trash. When Len had his opportunity in the NBA, Coach Reid told him he would be better off playing in Europe. When Len went to Europe he hated it. Once he didn't have basketball in his life he gave up."

"Do you know how I could find Len now? I need to find out what Reid had that made Len go to GCSU" Ced implored.

"No, I haven't spoken to Len in months. He couldn't or wouldn't hold a job. I tried to encourage him, but he started bringing people around the house that I didn't want around my other children. I told him I would help him, but he had to get a job and stop the drugs. I think he was selling drugs. When those criminals started showing up in my home I had to put my foot down. I told him to leave and not come back until he cleaned up his act."

Shirly Jo started weeping quietly. "I know I probably won't see him again in this life. I signed his death warrant, but I had no choice. He was killing himself and I couldn't let him kill my other babies with him. My other two children are both A students. They both have goals and dreams. It still hurts me to know I raised a son who is no different than his daddy. I realized I wouldn't want my daughter coming home with a boy like him. It is hard, but I had no choice. I told him to leave and haven't heard from him since."

Ced sat silently until Shirly Jo got back under control. He thanked her for telling him the story and told her he would try to find out what Ken Reid had done. Ced got up to leave.

"If you find my boy, would you tell him that his mama still loves him and wants him to come home? But only if he can clean himself up and get a job!"

Ced told her he would and left the home. As he drove away he tried to figure out how Ken Reid had convinced both Len Mallard and Tyron Washington to go to GCSU. What could he have had? Maybe he paid them? He would have to tell Matt about what he had learned then try to find Len Mallard.

CHAPTER SEVEN

Ced reported back to Matt on his findings. He really hadn't learned anything other than that Len Mallard didn't like Coach Reid, yet he had gone with him to GCSU. That made no sense so they had to find out the reason why. Ced told Matt he was going to stay in the area a few days to look for Len.

Matt decided he needed to find Tyron Washington. He had contacts throughout foreign basketball, but thought he better check in with Lisa Lasham at the NCAA before proceeding. Heaven forbid he should do something without the NCAA's approval!

Matt picked up the phone and dialed. Lisa answered on the first ring.

"Lisa Lasham speaking, may I help you?"

"Why I certainly hope so," Matt said. "This is Matt Colter. I'm wondering if you've had time to decide on the next step in the GCSU case?"

"Oh, hello Mr. Colter," Matt could hear the disappointment in Lisa's voice. He certainly had rubbed her the wrong way. That brought a smile to his face. He didn't know why he liked to dig at Lisa. He really did understand how difficult the enforcement job was, but he just had a thing for people who took themselves too seriously or abused their power or so-called power. Lisa had struck him as a person who took herself way too seriously and also as someone who liked the power that came with her position. That combination made Matt needle her whenever he saw an opportunity.

"So? Any thoughts about where you go next?" Matt asked.

"For your information," Lisa began, "I have conducted searches for both of the players. Their names are Tyron Washington and Len Mallard."

Matt was going to make a smart remark along the lines of what great investigative work, digging names out of a media guide, but he held back. Lisa continued.

"Washington is playing basketball in Turkey so we have no way to get ahold of him. I've spoken to our basketball focus group, but they don't have contacts in Turkey. Mallard has disappeared, no phone, no address, nothing. We think it is a dead end."

"So then I guess the case is closed?" Matt offered.

"Not even close! We still need to speak with Ken Reid. We think we have enough right now to take it to the Committee on Infractions."

Matt knew that Lisa was bluffing. This was just another display of someone who hadn't quite yet become comfortable in her position. She felt the need to bully trying to scare Matt. That made him laugh a little, which Lisa didn't like.

"You think this is funny?" Lisa asked.

"No, not funny. It is sort of sad, but I'll save my thoughts for another day."

"Good, I don't think you can spare any"

Matt smiled. He really had gotten to her. He decided to dig a little further.

"If you'd like, I can try to track down Tyron Washington. I have some contacts that might be able to help more than yours."

Before Lisa could object Matt continued. "As for Len Mallard, have you given any thought about talking to his family? Maybe they know his whereabouts."

Lisa seethed. Who did this guy think he was? He thought he had better contacts than the NCAA? That was laughable.

"Go ahead, I give you permission to try to track down both of them. I'll give you a week then you can call me back after you fail and we can then go talk to Ken Reid."

"Thanks for your permission," Matt replied sarcastically. "And what if I don't fail? What if I find Washington and/or Mallard?"

"Well then I guess I'll have to give you more credit. But I've used the full resources of the NCAA and came up empty so If you think you can do things the NCAA can't go ahead and try!"

Matt laughed again. "I'll see what I can come up with. You really need to learn to work with the other side when they extend an olive branch rather than let your pride get in the way. I'll get back to you before the end of this week."

With that Matt hung up the phone still laughing. He knew that Lisa was furious, but it would be a good learning experience for her. She took her job way too seriously.

It took Matt three hours to get Tyron Washington on the phone. The owner of his Greek team had called in a favor and Washington had called Matt shortly thereafter.

Matt explained what he was doing and that he represented GCSU. Washington told Matt that he didn't have fond memories of GCSU, but would be happy to do whatever necessary to get Ken Reid.

"So you don't like Ken Reid? Matt asked.

"Ken Reid is a devil who shouldn't be around kids" Washington responded.

Matt wanted to find out all he could, but refrained from immediately starting to question Tyron. Instead he explained that he needed to include the NCAA on the conversation. They agreed on a time for a conference call and hung up.

Matt called Lisa. It was four hours since their last conversation.

Again Lisa picked up on the first ring. She certainly was eager.

"Lisa Lasham speaking, may I help you?"

"Not so far, but I'm going to keep trying."

"Oh, hello Mr. Colter. What do you need now?"

"I don't need anything," Matt stated. "I'm calling to see if you want to take part in an interview with Tyron Washington tomorrow morning."

"You mean you actually got in touch with him? It's only been half a day!"

"Actually it was a little less than three hours. I must be getting rusty. Do you want to participate in the interview?"

"Of course," Lisa replied, then to save face she added, "So you couldn't find Len Mallard?"

"Mallard has left his home, but his mother was more than happy to talk."

Lisa was thoroughly defeated. This guy had tracked down and spoken to one of the players and the mother of the other player in three hours? She had greatly underestimated him! Matt could almost hear her deflate as she asked "so do we have an interview with Mallard's mom as well?"

"No, she already told us what she knew which wasn't much. She did say that her son hated Coach Reid."

"You mean you spoke to her without me present?"

Matt could hear Lisa start to puff up again over the phone.

"You really are something, do you know that?" he asked. "First you tell me that they are both unreachable, which I've shown to be more than false. Then you start to get upset because you weren't included in a conversation with the mother? All this after you told me you had all, but given up any hope of making contact? Go ahead and try to make that an issue. I would love to have that conversation in front of the Committee on Infractions."

Matt had gotten a little more upset than he had intended, but he thought it was time to set some boundaries and reign Lisa in a little bit. When she finally replied her tone was remorseful.

"I apologize, you are right. I shouldn't have gotten upset. What else did you learn from the Mallard mother?"

That was much better. Matt hoped she understood that he was just trying to help.

"Mrs. Mallard said that Len hated Ken Reid while they were at the junior college and she had no idea why he would go play for him at GCSU. She said Len never told her why he went there. Len developed a drug problem and she kicked him out of the house. She has no idea where he is."

"Do you believe her?"

Matt had no intention of telling Lisa that he had someone else working for him or that Ced was the one who had actually spoken to her. That was a secret he would keep in his back pocket. If Lisa believed Matt was the one who spoke with Shirly Jo Mallard, then he wouldn't correct her.

"Yes, she was very credible," Matt answered. "I'll keep trying to find Len Mallard, but I can't guarantee anything."

Matt gave Lisa the information about the call with Tyron Washington. The next morning all three were on the phone. Matt introduced Tyron to Lisa and told Tyron that Lisa would explain the NCAA procedures. Before he turned it over to Lisa he told Washington "remember, the NCAA can't do a thing to you. You aren't playing at an NCAA school any longer and unless you want to coach one day, you are outside their powers. Just be honest and straightforward and we'll see if we can figure out how to do the right thing here."

Lisa immediately jumped in, "Mr. Colter is right that you are outside of the NCAA powers as he calls them, but if you do ever want to coach at an NCAA school you must be truthful now. Right now you may have no intention of ever coaching, but who knows what the future brings?"

Washington interrupted her, "Listen, I am not real fond of the NCAA so please don't try to threaten me. I'm going to tell you what happened at one of your schools with one of your coaches," he emphasized the "your" both times. "I've moved on and am in a good place. Mr. Colter told me yesterday that you wanted to find out what Ken Reid did and I'm more than happy to tell you because I don't think he should be able to do to other kids what he did to us, so let's get started, but don't even think about threatening me again. If you do that again I hang up."

Matt was happy to hear that Tyron Washington wasn't intimidated by Lisa or the NCAA. Lisa continued on explaining the NCAA procedures and getting Washington's permission to record the interview. Once she was done with the preliminaries she began the questions.

"I guess the best thing to do is just to have you tell me the story of your basketball history. Tell us how you got to the junior college and then to GCSU."

Washington began his narration. He started with his high school career. He had played in Denver, Colorado and was all-state his junior year. The in-state schools Colorado and Colorado State along with Wyoming, Iowa and Iowa State had recruited him. He narrowed his choices to Colorado and Iowa, but then got hurt his senior year of high school. As soon as he got hurt, the schools recruiting him backed way off. When he finally was healed, he couldn't generate any interest. His dad had a friend who lived in North Dakota and told him about the JC there.

"My dad's friend contacted the head coach, Ken Reid. He gave him some film of me playing during my junior year, explained about my injury and told him I had completely recovered. Reid called me, we spoke about his style of play and the school. I just wanted to play so I agreed to go there and play for him."

Lisa asked a question, "did you get any type of financial aid at the junior college?"

Tyron told them that Reid had helped him get a job where he just showed up and sat in a room that had two security monitors. He was paid $25 an hour and was allowed to do his homework. "It wasn't a no show job, I had to be there, but I didn't do anything. I basically got paid to do my homework."

"Who paid you?" Matt asked.

"Some guy who was a friend of Reid's. He owned the place. He told me that I was there in case someone tried to break in and there was a phone for me to call the police if that happened. But the building I was in was empty. Nobody would ever try to break in because there was nothing in there except for me sitting in a chair watching the monitors. Reid had set up a few jobs like that, but we didn't talk about them on the team so I don't know who else was working those jobs."

"Okay, go on with the story," Lisa instructed.

Tyron told them how he had played his first year and done very well. He and Len Mallard were the best players on the team. They had finished first in their league and done well in the playoffs. Tyron told them that he had spoken with a counselor who told him which classes to take so that he could transfer to a four-year school. Everything was going well, except that the team didn't really like Coach Reid.

Tyron told them that Reid was cocky and rude to the players. He had coached at a Division I school and always reminded the team that he knew what it took to play at that level.

Tyron had finished up his first year with a 3.6 GPA. He was on track to get his AA degree and had already heard from a few four-year schools.

"When I started my second year, Coach Reid told me not to take the math course that my counselor had told me to take. Reid said that the teacher had it out for athletes, especially basketball players. He told both me and Len Mallard he would help us find a correspondence course that would satisfy the math requirement. We had heard some things about the teacher that weren't good so we went along with the plan."

"Our second season started and we did even better than the year before. I was scoring 24 points a game and Len Mallard was right behind me. Coach Reid found the math course and signed us both up."

"Did he sign you up or have you do it yourselves?" Lisa asked.

"That was an odd deal right there," Tyron answered. "Coach Reid was always very careful for us to fill out any paperwork in our own writing. He wouldn't even touch the papers with his bare hands. He always had someone else give them to us. We signed up for the classes, paid the money out of our own accounts and began getting the homework."

"So you paid for the classes?"

"Yes, I got a bonus at my job right around the time I had to sign up. The bonus covered the price of the course with a few dollars to spare."

"Did anyone tell you the bonus was to pay for the class?" Lisa asked.

"No, nobody ever said a word to me, but it was the only bonus I ever got and it came after we found out how much the class would cost. The class was $395 and my bonus was for $400. I don't think it takes a genius to figure out the connection, but to answer your question.... No, nobody ever said the bonus was to cover the cost of the class."

"Where was the material sent?" Matt questioned. "Did it come to the school, to your homes?"

"Oh no, Coach Reid had it mailed to the school. He wanted to be able to see it and get it, but didn't want it going to his home. I remember him saying something like this can't be traced back to me. We aren't doing anything wrong, but I don't want someone thinking I was telling you not to take the class offered at the school. He told us that he was looking out for our best interests. What a joke!"

"Why is that a joke?" Lisa replied. "It seems he was trying to help you find a class that worked better for you."

"Yes, it would appear that way wouldn't it?" Tyron said. "Let me tell you the rest of the story."

Tyron then explained that they struggled to do the work. It was an algebra class, which wasn't a strong subject for him or Len Mallard. Coach Reid had known that they would struggle so he had his wife meet with the players to tutor them. When we still didn't get it, Coach Reid came up with a plan. He had his wife do the first test we got. Then he had us copy it over in our own handwriting.

"I'm not gonna lie, I felt bad, but I had to pass that class to get my AA degree and transfer to a four-year school. But guess what happened on the way to our passing grade? We flunked the first test! His wife was a very nice lady, but she didn't know algebra any better than we did!"

"After we got those first tests back and saw that we had both gotten "F"s on them, Coach Reid came up with another plan. We had tutors for the basketball team. They were young girls just making extra money by helping us. Coach Reid used them without them ever knowing!

"He would get our homework then take it to the tutors and ask them to help us get through it. When it came time for the next test, Coach Reid got the test. He covered up where it said TEST by taping white paper over the word TEST and he photocopied it. He met with each tutor individually, but each of them thought they were the only one helping us. Coach Reid gave one tutor the even problems and the other the odd problems. He told the girls to do the problems he had given them. He told the one doing the even numbered problems that we had to do the odd problems. He said that we would review the even problems she had done and see how she worked them out. By reviewing her work we would be able to do the odd problems required by the class. Coach Reid then went to the other tutor and told her to do the odd numbered problems. He again, explained to her that we would review her work on the odd problems which would help us do the even numbered problems that were required by the class."

"And the girls had no idea what was going on?" Lisa asked.

"No idea whatsoever!" Tyron replied. "At the end, we would have both the odd and even problems finished. We would get the papers the girls had done and copy both the odd and even problems in our own handwriting onto the real test forms. Then Coach Reid would mail the tests back. He always made sure that we both missed a couple of problems so our grades weren't too high and it wasn't obvious that we were cheating."

Lisa was stunned by this. Matt was thinking ahead and asked, "didn't you have a final exam? Usually these classes have a final that has to be proctored by a real teacher of some sort. Did this class require a final?"

Tyron laughed, "You are good! Yes, there was a final exam. I was nervous about it because I knew I couldn't do the work, but Coach Reid told us he had it covered. We went to the home of one of the professor's on campus. Coach Reid came with us. He brought along a packet that had the final exam in it. Coach Reid gave us the final along with the even and odd problems completed by the tutors."

"Wait," Matt interrupted. "Most of those final exams come in sealed packets and are only to be opened by the proctor. Are you saying that Coach

Reid opened them in advance and had the tutors do the same odd/even thing. Didn't the professor object?"

"The professor never even looked at the paperwork. Coach Reid brought a case of beer with him. After Coach Reid gave us the paperwork and told us to sit on opposite sides of the room, he and the professor went into the other room to watch basketball and drink beers. I remember him saying that they would leave the door open to make sure we didn't cheat. They started the timer and left us alone."

"Did the girls, the tutors, know it was the final exam? Wouldn't they have seen the final exam material and known something was up?" Lisa wondered out loud.

"No, because Coach Reid never told them it was a final exam. They thought it was another homework assignment because he covered up the heading of the test and anything that mentioned final exam before making copies, which he gave to the tutors. When we got to the professor's house he gave us the final exam, then gave us the papers the tutors had done. I sat there and copied their answers and work because we had to show our work on the final. When we finished we sealed it all up in the envelope and took the extra paperwork the tutors had done and stuffed them into our backpacks. We told Coach Reid we were done and he had the professor collect the tests."

"What kinds of grades did you get on the final?" Lisa asked.

"I got a 94 percent and Len got an 88 percent. I don't know how he missed that many, but it was probably good he did."

"Do you have any proof of this?" Matt asked. "Don't get mad, but right now it is your word against Coach Reid's. We need someone else to corroborate your story. We can't find Len Mallard. Who else would be able to tell us about this?"

You could almost hear Tryon thinking over the phone. "I get what you are saying. The tutors don't know anything about this. The professor sure isn't going to admit to anything because he most likely would get fired over it. Coach Reid's wife would be embarrassed to admit she couldn't do the work. I don't know who else could back me up, sorry."

While Matt didn't like the answer, he thought that Tyron's honesty made him much more believable.

"Okay, let us worry about that for now," Lisa stated. "This still doesn't explain why you both followed Coach Reid to GCSU. In fact it makes it even more unbelievable that you did follow him."

"That is why I call him a snake. It is bad enough that he got us to cheat. We thought he was doing it so we would stay eligible and make him look like a better coach than he really was. What makes him completely despicable is what happened after we got our grades in the Algebra class. We were both being recruited by a number of schools. Coach Reid called us into his office and told us he had a chance to become an assistant at GCSU, but it was important that we go with him. We both told him we weren't interested in doing that."

"I still remember it like it was yesterday. Coach Reid stood up and said that he needed us to do him that favor. He told us that we would lose our eligibility and be banned from ever playing in the NCAA if word got out that we had cheated on our algebra course. He said that nothing could be traced back to him since it was all done in our own handwriting. He told us that an anonymous call to the NCAA would end our college careers before they started."

"Looking back, I wonder what I was thinking. Of course he would have gone down with us, but at the time all I wanted to do was play college basketball. We went along with him because we thought we had no choice."

There was silence on the phone for about ten seconds.

Matt finally broke the silence by asking "did you ever tell anyone at that time what had happened? Did you tell a family member, friend or girlfriend?"

"I don't know about Len Mallard, but I never said a word to anyone. How could I? I would have been exposed as a cheater. Nope, we followed Coach Reid, who we detested, to GCSU and helped him further his career. I don't know if I could have played in the NBA, but I would have liked to have been coached by a good coach and seen what happened. Now I'll never know. I hope you get Coach Reid."

They concluded the conversation asking various questions then Lisa terminated the call. After they hung up, she called Matt right back.

"Okay, now do you agree GCSU has some serious problems?"

"I don't think you have anything that links this back to GCSU other than Ken Reid was hired by them. Nothing here links this in any way to GCSU or shows that anyone from GCSU was involved. You may have Ken Reid, but you still need someone to corroborate this story. If you get that he will never coach again and that would be a good thing. Are you going to follow up by trying to speak with the tutors or the professor at the JC?"

"I think we have more than enough right now," Lisa responded. "Besides, Tyron was right, the tutors don't know anything and the professor isn't going to just confess to his role in the cheating."

"But don't you owe it to the investigation to at least give him a chance to tell his version?"

"No, the enforcement staff has been charged with bringing these cases to conclusion more quickly. I think we have enough. I'm going to start writing the notice of charges. You can tell GCSU that they should expect something in the next few weeks."

Matt couldn't believe she wasn't going to follow up. This wasn't the NCAA he knew. "I'm going to try to track down the tutors and the professor. My client will want to know the full story, not just a part of it."

"That is fine by me," Lisa stated. "They should take the time to understand their failings."

Matt hung up exasperated by Lisa's attitude. He probably wouldn't get anything more that would help, but GCSU might want to bring a lawsuit against Coach Reid so he had to talk to everyone.

CHAPTER EIGHT

After explaining what he had learned to president Scott at GCSU, Matt made preparations to travel to North Dakota. He had to track down the tutors, but knew it would take some hard work and a bit of luck since they had left the JC three years ago.

It turned out that Coach Reid had blazed a trail that played a big part in Matt successfully tracking down the tutors. The trail came in the form of the head of the tutoring department at the junior college. Matt went to her office the first thing after checking into his hotel. He had debated what information to give to her, but decided full disclosure might be the best tactic here.

So Matt explained who he was, what he was doing and why he needed to find the tutors. When he told her he was looking into Coach Reid, she immediately lit up and said "I'll do anything I can to get the slimeball."

It turned out that the head of the tutoring department and Coach Ken Reid had their share of run-ins through the years. That was very fortunate for Matt because she was still in contact with the former tutors. She said she would speak to the former tutors and see if they would be willing to talk. She suggested that Matt let her contact them initially because they would be more willing to talk if she prepped them. "Trust me sir, they are going to talk, but you have to let me approach them."

Matt decided he had no choice so he let her make the initial calls. He gave her his cell phone number and went back to his hotel. It only took an hour for her to call him. She asked him to come back to her office as soon as he could. He told her he would be there in ten minutes.

When he showed up she handed him a piece of paper with both of the former tutor's names, addresses and phone numbers. "I told them you might want to contact them in person and they both agreed to meet with you. You need to call them to set up appointments to meet with them, but they are both ready to talk. Neither of them liked Coach Reid either!"

Matt was pleasantly surprised at how quickly this woman had gotten things done. He thanked her profusely. As he walked towards the door to leave she stopped him.

"One more thing. Coach Reid's ex-wife is a good friend of mine. I didn't say anything to her, but you might want to contact her to see if she knows anything about what you are doing. She may not want to talk, but I know he has hurt her tremendously. Here is her address, but please don't tell her you got it from me. I've been very supportive of her throughout the divorce. The only reason I'm giving you her address and telling you this is because I think it might be cathartic for her."

Matt again thanked her. He got in his car and then looked over the information the woman had given him. The tutor's names were Trina Coker and Shelby Astle. Both had graduated from the junior college. Trina was enrolled at UCLA in Los Angeles and Shelby had gone to Loyola Marymount, also in Los Angeles. It looked like Matt would have to schedule a trip to Los Angeles, but he couldn't do it this week. Matt took out his phone and dialed Trina Coker. She agreed to meet with Matt the following week.

Matt then called Shelby Astle. She listened to what Matt had to say. Matt could tell she was much more hesitant to talk with him. Matt gave her a little more information and finally she agreed to meet, but only if her father could be present during the conversation. Matt told her that would be no problem and he would welcome having her father there. He scheduled both appointments for the same day the following week.

With that wrapped up so quickly, Matt decided to push his luck. He went to the address of Reid's ex-wife. Her name was Kaitlyn. Matt didn't know what he was going to say, but thought he could at least ask her about her helping with the algebra courses. He pulled into a condominium complex, parked the car and climbed the stairs to 3D, the number of her condo. He knocked three times then waited.

A woman answered the door, but only opened it a crack with a chain firmly in place. Matt asked if Kaitlyn Reid lived there.

"Who is asking?" the woman wanted to know.

Matt explained who he was and passed his business card through the narrow opening. The woman took the card, looked at it for a while then sighed and said, "hold on".

She shut the door, unlatched the chain then opened the front door. Before Matt could speak she started in.

"Look, Ken and I are finally divorced. If he owes you money then you need to find him, not me."

"Why would you think Ken owed me money?" Matt asked.

"Well you are an attorney. Aren't you here for a client looking for Ken?"

"No, I think I better explain. I have been hired by Grand Central State University to represent them in an NCAA investigation. I just need to ask you a few questions if I could."

Kaitlyn thought about that for a moment. Finally she spoke.

"Tell me exactly what it is you want to know and I'll decide if I think I can help or not. I don't want to get question after question so give them all to me now and let me decide."

Matt didn't like it, but he had no choice. He explained the entire story to her. Then he told her that he wanted to know if she would confirm what Tyron had told him.

"Those poor boys, Tyron and Len. Ken really screwed them. They weren't bad kids. Both of them used to come over to the house and they were so sweet. My daughter was just two at the time and they would both play with her and entertain her. She loved their visits. She used to light up when they came over. They were just big kids themselves."

"So you'll help me?" Matt asked.

"I'm sorry, I can't. The story you told me is true, but I can't officially go on the record. I just worked out the final divorce agreement. Ken gave me full custody of my daughter with him having limited visitation rights. My daughter adores her daddy and I won't do anything that would hurt that. I feel badly for those boys, but I have to think of my daughter first."

Matt knew it was useless to try to talk her out of her position. He could see the determination in her eyes so he didn't try. Matt sincerely believed that family was more important than his job. It was one of the things that made him different than most of the attorneys who were involved in this line of work.

"I completely understand. At the end of the day this isn't life and death, it is just sports. You have family to think about and your daughter should always come first. Here is my card, if you think of anything that might help me or know of someone else I could speak with let me know. I won't bother you again and good luck with your daughter."

Kaitlyn looked startled. "You mean that is it? You aren't going to try to convince me?"

"I don't think it would do any good," Matt stated. "I understand the position you are in. You might be able to provide some information that would help Tyron and Len, but it may harm your daughter. I get that and not only do I get it, I agree with you. I will find the information somewhere else. You are a good mother and I wouldn't do anything that might make you second-guess yourself later. Thanks again."

Matt turned and walked back to his car with Kaitlyn Reid staring at him the whole way. He waved as he drove away. He went back to the hotel, grabbed his things and barely made a late flight back home. Rushing around, chasing down leads, hotels and airlines were Matt's life. He enjoyed doing different things every day, but it sure was exhausting. It was Tuesday and he had other things to do the rest of the week so he would fly to Los Angeles next Sunday. He had everything nicely planned, but those plans never quite work out as he envisioned and this would be no exception.

Wednesday was a normal day, with not much happening, but Thursday morning the Federal Express man showed up with a big cardboard box for Matt. Since he wasn't expecting anything he was very interested in what it might be. He signed for it and noticed that the box came from North Dakota.

Matt ripped open the box and saw it was full of papers. He took out the papers noticing a note on the top. The note said:

Mr. Colter, I thought about those two boys and what my husband did to them. I decided I had to do right by them because they have mothers. What type of mother would I be if I turned my back on them? If there is any way you can protect me I would appreciate it, but I know that might not be possible so let the chips fall where they may. I won't sit for an interview, but I will give you paperwork showing what happened. You'll find the proof that those boys took a correspondence algebra course. I don't know why I kept this. You will find the tests the boys "took" and their grades on the tests. I have also included papers showing the work two tutors did without knowing they were doing anything wrong. My ex-husband covered up the top of each test and made copies of them. The tutors never knew they were doing the work for the actual test so please don't blame them. He told them it was just practice homework for the test, but you can see where it is blank across the top of the papers the tutors did. I'm done with it and won't talk to anyone about it so don't try to contact me. Good luck and thanks for reminding me what is really important.

Matt was stunned. He perused the paperwork and saw the tests, the photocopies of the tests with the word TEST covered over. A quick look showed that the two tests had handwriting that Matt presumed was the writing of Len and Tyrone. The writing on the photocopies was very different and looked to be feminine in nature. Anyone could tell it had been done by someone else. Matt had the proof he needed to confront Ken Reid. Now he needed to talk to the tutors.

CHAPTER NINE

Matt spent the next few days getting ready to go to Los Angeles for his interviews with the tutors. He hadn't heard from Ced in a few days and arranged to meet him for lunch upon arriving into town. Matt wasn't worried about Ced, but he did wonder what else Ced had found during his stay in L.A.

Matt toyed with calling Lisa at the NCAA to let her know what he had obtained in the Fed Ex package, but decided against it. She hadn't been interested enough to do any of the work so she shouldn't reap the rewards. Matt still wasn't sure exactly how this played into the NCAA investigation.

Matt thought about what they knew up to now. It appeared that Ken Reid had blackmailed his players, Tyron Washington and Len Mallard, into attending GCSU so he would be hired as an assistant coach, but there was no indication that anyone from GCSU had been involved in any way. Since Ken Reid was employed at a junior college at the time, Matt wasn't sure if it even fit under NCAA rules or under NCAA jurisdiction.

The argument could be made that since the algebra grades appeared to not have been earned legitimately, then Tyron and Len were not eligible to compete for GCSU, but GCSU had no knowledge of that, at least on the surface. Once Ken Reid became employed at GCSU, he had an obligation under NCAA rules to inform GCSU and the NCAA, which of course he didn't do.

Matt wasn't sure how this was going to all shake out, but he knew he had a mess on his hands. When he got into these types of situations, his policy had been to just keep plowing forward and eventually it would all work itself out one way or another. Just find the truth and let that guide the next steps.

Knowing that GCSU was looking to perhaps rid itself of its men's basketball coaching staff, Matt thought there was ample evidence that Ken Reid had done something wrong, but didn't think there was any proof that either Randy Culp or Ned McEnroe had been involved. Matt would have to keep digging to see what he could uncover. If Randy and Ned were innocent, then Matt had no problem telling President Scott.

Matt landed in Los Angeles and rode the shuttle bus to get his rental car. It always took so long in Los Angeles from the time the plane landed until you actually drove out of the rental car lot. Then you hit the 405 freeway and the immediate traffic that is a constant in Los Angeles. It took over an hour from the time Matt deplaned until he finally turned off the 405 onto the 91 freeway. He met Ced at a Mexican restaurant that Ced had recommended.

Matt entered the restaurant and found Ced chatting up the hostess and two of the servers. They were all laughing as Ced told stories. Matt almost hated to interrupt, but Ced saw Matt and waved him over.

"This is the guy I was telling you about. I better get down to business."

Matt didn't know what Ced had been telling them, but for all Matt knew Ced had been telling them about when he played against the Lakers and not even talking about Matt. Ced often did things like that just to tease Matt.

They were seated and soon ordered their meal. Matt ordered a chicken burrito while Ced ordered the Enchilada platter and a few side tacos. They munched on chips and salsa while they waited for their food.

"I've got a lead on Len Mallard, but he isn't staying in any one place. He is currently homeless, but is selling drugs to lowlifes down by the Long Beach Aquarium. The city and police have done a great job making it a safe place so Len isn't having much success. I've let some people know that I want to talk to him and I may have to give him a little motivation to sit down with me."

Matt never paid witnesses and Ced knew that. Matt started to mention that, but Ced interrupted him before he could begin.

"I know that you wouldn't want me to pay him and I'm not going to pay him for his testimony, but I may buy him a meal to sit down with me then I'm going to try to get him into rehab. His mother is a very nice lady and I owe it to her to at least try. Is his testimony vital to your case?"

Matt thought that over. In reality, Len's testimony wasn't really needed, but would cement what Tyron told him.

"I don't think we need his testimony, but you never know. If you could get him to open up to you a little bit it wouldn't hurt. Approach him with the theme that you are after Ken Reid. So far I haven't found anyone who liked Ken Reid except maybe for Randy Culp, but that isn't surprising because coaches usually stick together. Once you see if you can get Len to talk to you then you can push for rehab and I'll be happy to pick up the tab. Does that work?"

Ced smiled his big smile and said "okay I'll see what I can do".

Matt filled Ced in on what Tyron had told them and also what Ken Reid's wife had said. When Matt told Ced about the Fed Ex package and the proof of the academic fraud, Ced laughed a great big laugh.

"Nothing worse than a woman scorned!"

They enjoyed a great California Mexican lunch. Matt knew that when he traveled to the west coast he could always count on finding good Mexican food, which he really enjoyed. With a full stomach, he parted company with Ced. Matt headed back towards downtown Los Angeles for his interview with Trina Coker.

Coker was a student at UCLA so Matt had agreed to meet her in Westwood at a Starbucks. Westwood was a popular hangout of UCLA students. Matt didn't like meeting in such a public place, but he had no choice. He couldn't meet Coker at her apartment in this day and age. There were too many risks for both of them. Coker didn't know Matt and was smart enough to not let a strange man into her apartment. Matt didn't know Coker and was smart enough to not arrange to meet a woman alone in her apartment, so Starbucks it was.

Luckily, it was mid afternoon so Starbucks wasn't real busy. Matt found a little table in the corner and waited. Soon a short young girl walked in and loudly said "Is Matt Colter here?"

Matt chuckled at her direct approach and he waved to her. She walked over and sat down.

"Hello, I'm Trina Coker. I'm sorry for being so loud, but I didn't want to look around trying to guess who you were."

"No problem," Matt said. "I should have figured out some identifying signal. Would you like something to drink? My treat."

"Oh I don't drink coffee, but maybe I'll get a hot chocolate if that is okay?"

"Sure, order away."

They both stood in line and Trina ordered a hot chocolate while Matt got a juice from the cooler. Matt paid for both and then they sat back down.

"Juice? Do you think we are the first people who ever came into a Starbucks and didn't order coffee?" Trina asked.

"I don't know, I don't drink coffee either so I rarely come into a Starbucks," Matt stated.

"Why don't you drink coffee?" Trina asked. "I would expect an attorney to put in a lot of late nights and need some stimulation to keep awake."

"I don't want to bore you with my history, but let's just say that I'm not one to put things into my body that may be harmful and I put caffeine into that category. I'd rather be a little tired than have to rely on caffeine to keep me awake. I know that is not normal, but I'm happy with my choice."

"Wow, I thought I was the only one! My roommates take caffeine pills to stay up late studying so I decided to quit any artificial stimulants including coffee. Not only have I saved a ton of money, but I feel healthier than I did when I was drinking a couple of cups of coffee a day. But I guess you don't want to talk about coffee, do you?"

Again Matt chuckled. This young lady was very direct, but Matt found himself liking her quite a bit. It was obvious that she didn't need any caffeine! She was small, but full of energy. Matt thought she probably could accomplish whatever she put her mind to. He explained what he was doing and touched a little bit on Ken Reid.

"Oh, I didn't like Coach Reid at all," Trina interrupted. "He gave me the creeps, but I could never put my finger on the reason why. He never said anything really forward, but I always had the feeling that he would have welcomed any physical contact if I initiated it. When Shelby and I were tutors for the basketball team we used to talk about it. The players were all very nice, but neither of us liked dealing with Coach Reid."

Matt told her he was focusing on Tyron Washington and Len Mallard and the help that Trina and Shelby provided to them.

"Tyron was one of the nicest guys on the team. He was always very polite and thanked me whenever I helped him. Len was much quieter and I got a sense that he struggled more socially than Tyron did. Why are you asking about them? Did they do something wrong?" Trina asked. "Both of them were very nice to me and to Shelby."

"No, I don't think you did anything wrong, but I need to get your story and then I'll explain the whole situation to you. Do you mind if I record you? I just need you to walk me through what happened. I may interrupt and ask questions, but basically I just want you to tell me what you remember from that time."

Trina agreed to tell what she could remember so Matt started the recorder, gave some introductory comments then had Trina start talking. She talked and talked only slowing down to take a sip of her hot chocolate every so often. She walked through how she was hired as a tutor and was assigned to the men's basketball team. Her work consisted mostly of helping the players with math homework and trying to get them to understand the concepts. Occasionally she would help them with homework from other classes, but her specialty was math.

She then told how Coach Reid had asked her to help Tyron and Len with a correspondence algebra course. She recalled how Coach Reid had told her that the correspondence course required the players to do the even problems on the homework so he asked her if she would do the odd problems to show the players how to do the work.

Matt interrupted at this point. "How sure are you that he had you do the odd problems?"

"Oh, I'm 100 percent sure, because I remember thinking it was odd that I was doing only the odd problems! Get it, odd doing the odd? I remember that vividly, but since it was the Coach asking and not the players I didn't think much more about it."

Trina explained that Coach Reid would bring the homework to her and then collect it from her a day or two later.

"Did you ever talk directly with the players themselves?" Matt asked.

"I usually try to get to know the people I'm tutoring a little bit. It helps me better understand why they might be struggling. With Tyron and Len, I had talked to them before when they came for help with other subjects. I remember Tyron being very polite. I would say he was very gentlemanly and nice. Len was quieter. I never really got to know him at all. Once I started helping with the algebra class I never spoke with either one of them or talked to them directly about their homework. I always dealt with Coach Reid."

"Didn't that seem odd to you?" Matt questioned. "I mean, you were talking with the players all the time, then suddenly you were only talking with the coach. That wasn't how you normally worked so how come you didn't question it?"

Trina thought for a moment then said, "well when you say it like that I guess I should have questioned it, but at the time, I probably thought since it was the coach asking about a correspondence course maybe it was a little different. I don't really know. I guess I just trusted the adult in charge, but now I'm thinking I should have asked more questions."

Matt pulled out the paperwork he had received in the fed ex package. He found the papers he had received from Kaitlyn Reid. He slid the copied over final exam to Trina. The top was just blank with problems beginning about a third of the way down the page. He had two copies, one with the odd problems completed and one with the even problems completed.

"Does any of this look familiar to you?" Matt asked.

Trina looked over the paperwork.

"This looks like the homework assignments I worked on," Trina said sliding a stack of papers back to Matt. "I did the odd problems, like I told you. That is my writing. I can tell by how the numbers are formed. I draw my threes and fours in a very distinct manner so I'm sure these are mine. These other papers, with the even numbers completed, I would have thought were the papers completed by of the players, but the handwriting looks feminine."

She looked at a while longer in silence then looked at Matt.

"I think I get what happened. I bet Shelby did this one, didn't she? I can't believe I was so stupid. Coach Reid had me do the odd problems and Shelby do the even ones didn't he? Then he took them to the Tyrone and Len to copy. Is that what this is all about?"

Matt didn't want to confirm anything so he sat in silence while she looked at the papers.

"I don't recall ever talking to Shelby about this. Did Coach Reid set us up to do something illegal? Am I going to get in trouble for helping them cheat?"

Matt couldn't believe how quickly Trina grasped exactly what had happened.

"I can't tell you for sure, but we are definitely looking at this correspondence course and trying to figure out how things worked. You have confirmed one part of it for me. I don't think you did anything wrong. You may have been taken advantage of, but I don't think you knew anything about it.

We have already gotten the story from someone and you have now confirmed a piece of it for me. Can you do me a favor?"

"Sure, what do you need?" Trina sat there looking stunned.

"I don't know if you still have contact with Shelby, but could you please not contact her until I have a chance to speak with her? Give me a day then you can talk to her all you want. I think I'm going to get to the bottom of this, but I need to talk to everyone privately before they all start comparing stories. I'd appreciate it if you and Shelby would just sit tight until I have a chance to wrap this all up."

Trina still sat staring at the paperwork. Matt could tell she was thinking it through trying to work though everything in her mind. He felt badly for her so touched her arm.

"Look, don't take this too hard. You were an innocent young girl who had no reason to suspect that a coach would direct you to do something wrong. I see things like this all the time. This won't come back to harm you in any way. Just learn from it and go forward with your life. Don't let it worry you. Here is my card, call me any time and once we get a resolution I'll let you know. Thanks for taking the time to meet with me."

Trina kept looking at the papers. Matt could tell she was trying to remember more about the class. She suddenly told him, "I never realized it until this moment, but Coach Reid never spoke to Shelby and me at the same time about this class. I realize now that he talked only with me about doing the odd problems. Sometimes Shelby and I would work together so we made sure all of the material was covered or one of us would communicate to the other if a student was struggling in a specific area. I don't have any memories of ever talking to Shelby about this class."

"Why is that odd? Weren't there a lot of times you didn't speak with Shelby about a student you were helping?"

"Oh sure," Trina replied. "We didn't share everything except when it came to the basketball team. That was handled differently. We communicated everything to make sure things were covered. But Coach Reid asked me to help with the correspondence course and I remember him telling me that he only wanted one person helping with that. I just took that to mean me and that I shouldn't mention it to anyone else."

"Why would it be wrong to mention it?" Matt asked.

"Maybe I thought Coach Reid using the correspondence course was bending a rule since we taught the course at the junior college. I don't really know, but I never did tell Shelby I was helping the players with that class. Now I know why."

Matt stood up and Trina followed his lead. Matt shook hands with Trina and thanked her for meeting with him. He told her he would get to the bottom of this and would keep her out of it. Trina walked out of the Starbucks mumbling to herself. Matt could tell she was the type of person who would have to work through all of this, but he hoped she would get to the end of the problem in her mind and then move on with her life.

He had one piece of the puzzle confirmed, now he had to do the same thing with Shelby Astle. Coach Reid was leaving a long line of angry people in his wake.

CHAPTER TEN

It is a short drive from UCLA to the campus of Loyola Marymount University, but in Los Angeles, that drive can take over an hour in heavy traffic, and when is there not heavy traffic? Matt left plenty of time to spare for his drive to meet Shelby Astle.

Shelby had mentioned that her father would want to sit in on the discussion so Matt was prepared to take some time to explain to the father what Matt was doing. Matt wasn't prepared for the full force that was Mr. Astle!

Matt had arranged to meet Shelby at her apartment. Since her father would be there, he didn't have the same reservations he would have had about meeting Trina Coker at her apartment.

Shelby lived near the Los Angeles airport in an older, but nice area. Matt was able to find a parking spot on the street a couple of buildings down from where Shelby lived. He parked his car and walked to her building. He went up the stairs and knocked.

A very large man opened the door looking down on Matt. Matt wasn't small, but he felt small as he looked up into the man's face. The man easily stood 6 foot 6 and the word "burly" would be a good description. He filled the doorway and seemed massive.

"You must be Matt Colter, I'm Buck Astle," the man said. "Come in, come in."

The man stepped back with a flourish allowing Matt to enter. The apartment wasn't large, but with Matt and Buck Astle in the same room, it was very crowded.

"Sit down in that chair," Buck said, pointing to a wingback chair near the window. Matt walked over and sat down while Buck backed up to the couch and plopped down. It was only after Buck sat down that Matt realized there was another person in the room. Sitting next to Buck on the couch was the most beautiful girl that Matt had ever seen. She had long blonde hair and a smile that lit up the room.

"Matt Colter, this is my daughter Shelby," Buck introduced them.

"I'm pleased to meet you Shelby and I want to thank you both for taking the time to meet with me. I hope this won't take too long, but as I mentioned on the phone, I have some questions I'm trying to get answered and I was told you would be a good person to speak with."

Before Shelby could even begin to respond Buck sat forward.

"I don't want to be a pain to you or hinder what you are trying to accomplish, but before Shelby speaks to you, I have some questions I need answered. If you answer them fully then she'll talk, but if you equivocate in any way you'll need to get a court order for her to speak to you. Are we clear?"

Matt didn't want to get off on the wrong foot and he knew Buck was only protecting his daughter so he smiled.

"Mr. Astle, we are crystal clear! I'll answer any questions you have, but perhaps I should start by explaining in greater depth what this is all about?"

Buck sat back and smiled a huge smile.

"That is exactly what I wanted you to say. I'm usually a pretty good judge of character and I thought I'd like you when I opened the door. You could have pulled out the attorney card and tried to be all official, but instead you open up and offer to give us an explanation. That is perfect so go ahead and explain and we'll follow up with any questions we have."

Matt, too, was relieved. He explained what he was doing, gave some information about what he had learned, being careful to not provide too much information that might color Shelby's interview.

When Matt got to the part of his story that involved Tyron and Len, he hesitated for a moment.

"Why are you stopping here?" Buck asked. "Do you think Shelby did something wrong?" Buck turned to look at his daughter. "Shelby, you told me you didn't do anything wrong, does this man have information that will make me think differently?"

"No, daddy!" Shelby spoke for the first time. "I swear I didn't do anything wrong. I do know Tyron and Len, but all I did was help them, I promise!"

Buck looked sternly at his daughter. He had a force about him that was so powerful that Matt couldn't imagine anyone ever lying to this large man.

"Mr. Astle, I don't think your daughter did anything wrong. I think someone may have not been honest with her, but I can't tell you about that until I hear from your daughter. Once I get her full story I'll fill you in on the details I can't talk about right now."

They all paused and looked at each other for a moment. Matt waited on Buck Astle, because clearly he was the one making the decisions in the room. After what seemed like an eternity, but was in reality only about 30 seconds, Buck nodded at his daughter and told her to go ahead and answer Matt's questions.

Matt took the moment to speak up.

"Shelby, again, I don't think you have done anything wrong. I want to be clear at the outset that I think you performed your job as instructed, but I don't think you got all of the information. I'd like to record this interview so I have an accurate record and also, so I can provide a copy to the NCAA if it is needed. Are you both okay with that?"

Matt asked Shelby, but he looked at Buck as he formed the question because he knew Buck would make the decision.

"We have no problem with you recording this, but I hope you would allow us the same opportunity?" Buck said as he pulled out his own recording device and smiled. "It never hurts to be prepared now does it?"

Matt laughed out loud then told Buck he had no problem with Buck recording the interview as well.

Matt turned on his recorder allowing Buck to do the same. Matt then took a moment to get on the record the date and location of the interview. He also stated the reason for the interview. With that out of the way he started the questioning by simply saying, "Shelby, I understand you were a tutor for the men's basketball team at the junior college you attended in North Dakota?"

Shelby nodded, but before Matt could say anything Buck jumped in.

"Shelby, honey, you have to talk. The recorders can't pick up that you are nodding in agreement."

Shelby smiled. Matt again, thought she was the most beautiful young woman he had ever met. She had a perfect smile.

"I'm sorry, Mr. Colter, yes that is correct. I was one of the tutors for the basketball team."

"What I'd like for you to do is tell me your duties as a tutor and then walk me through your interactions with the players with special emphasis on any interaction you had with Tyron Washington and Len Mallard."

Shelby thought for a moment then began.

"I was hired in the middle of my first term by the academic advising department to tutor students. My English professor said it would be a good way to make a little money and help others. I was originally hired to tutor in English, but then started helping with math as well."

Buck leaned forward, interrupting his daughter. "Shelby is a great student. She had scholarship offers to a number of the Ivy schools, but she ran into a problem her last year in high school. A man she didn't even know started stalking her. We got restraining orders, but he didn't care and the police couldn't guarantee her safety. Rather than send her off to an Ivy League school, where I couldn't protect her 24/7, we decided to send her to North Dakota. I have an uncle who teaches at the junior college. I thought that maybe a year there, hidden from this man, would calm the situation and allow Shelby to resume a normal life. You have to understand that this man even scared me a little bit and I don't scare easily. This guy wasn't just obsessed, he had a threatening aura about him that was way out there."

Matt thought that he should pause the recording since this had nothing to do with his case, but Buck kept charging forward so Matt simply sat and listened while Buck continued.

"Sure enough, the man searched everywhere for Shelby. He even sent me threatening letters, but I kept her from contacting me and didn't allow her to use credit cards or social media. About four months after Shelby went to North Dakota, the man tried to break into my home. I called the police. I thought I would have to kill the man myself. but one of the police officers confronted him outside of my home. The man drew a gun so the officer ended up shooting and killing the man.

"Shelby stayed for one year in North Dakota. She considered going back east, but decided to stay near home, which made me happier. I just thought you should have that background so you will understand why I'm a little overprotective."

"Mr. Astle, I appreciate you sharing that with me," Matt began. "I had no idea and hope this hasn't caused either of you any more anxiety. I feel terribly that you have gone through all of that and now here I am hitting you with something else."

Matt really did feel badly. He realized that both Shelby and Buck had been through a lot and didn't like adding to it.

Shelby smiled at Matt.

"Mr. Colter, you had no way of knowing so don't worry about it. I'm fine. Now where was I? Oh yes, I started tutoring regular students then was asked if I wanted to be assigned to the basketball team. I thought it might be fun so I agreed. I provided help to any of the players that needed help in English and Math, but I ended up helping them in any subjects in which they needed assistance.

"It was fun because they were funny! Now you asked specifically about Tyron and Len. Tyron was probably the nicest of the bunch. He was very polite and always thanked me for helping him. I thought of them as friends and everything was great. Then one day Coach Reid came to me and asked me to help Tyron and Len with a correspondence course they were taking. He said that they were struggling without a teacher and needed to visualize what they were doing. I remember him coming up with the idea of me doing the even problems because they only had to do the odd problems for the class. He said if they could see how I worked out the even problems it would help them understand how to do the work for the ones that they had to turn in."

Matt interrupted her. "Was Trina Coker there when Coach Reid asked you to do the even problems?"

Shelby answered right away.

"No, I'm sure she wasn't there. I remember that Coach Reid asked me to not tell Trina because he didn't want her to be offended that he asked me. He said everyone knew I was the smartest of the tutors so he only wanted me to do it and didn't want Trina to be hurt."

"So then you would do the even problems and give them back to Tyron and Len?" Matt asked.

"I worked directly with the players most of the time, but for that correspondence course, I only gave things directly to Coach Reid. I think he was worried that since it wasn't a class being taught at the school that maybe the school wouldn't cover the tutoring payments if someone found out. I just assumed that is why he didn't have the players talk to me directly about it."

Matt pulled out the paperwork and found the final exam that had been covered up. He found the paper with the even problems completed and showed it to Shelby.

"Does this look familiar?"

Buck leaned over to look at the paperwork. Shelby started nodding her head and said "I can't be sure, but this looks like one of the assignments that Coach Reid gave to me to complete. This writing is mine so I'm sure it was one of the homework assignments, but I don't remember which one it was."

"So were all of the homework assignments like this?"

Shelby thought it over for a few minutes before answering.

"I think there were about ten assignments like this, but this was by far the longest one. Most were about ten to twenty problems, but as you can see, this one has about four times as many. I think this was towards the end of the class because most of the assignments were on one topic and this one was sort of a review of the entire class."

Buck looked at the paper. Matt could see he was confused, but he wasn't quite yet ready to fill him in on what had happened.

"Shelby, did you ever hear about Tyron or Len taking tests in that class? Did they ever talk to about taking tests?"

"Like I said, I didn't really talk to them about this class. I helped them with other classes taught at our school and we would talk about the teachers, but I never talked to either one of them about this class. I just thought Coach Reid didn't want me to get in trouble for tutoring in a class that wasn't part of the junior college or something like that. He seemed sort of nervous about my help with this class, but I don't think there was anything wrong. I just helped them as he asked me to."

Matt asked a few more questions then concluded the interview. As soon as he turned off his recorder Buck Astle sprang into action.

"Okay, I'm not sure what happened with this class, but it all sounds very fishy to me. What is going on with all of this and how is Shelby involved?"

Matt told Buck and Shelby that he wasn't 100% sure, even though he would have wagered quite a bit that he was spot on with what happened. He told them what he had learned and that it appeared that Coach Reid had figured out a way for Tyron and Len to get the work done by Shelby and Trina.

Buck started turning red. "You mean he used my daughter to help those boys cheat?"

Matt didn't want to give the whole story away so he didn't try to explain that it appeared that Coach Reid used that class to make the players go with him to his new job. He thought it would be better if Buck didn't know everything until it got resolved.

"What I can tell you Mr. Astle is that Shelby and Trina's names will not be brought into this. We've still got quite a bit to figure out and both Tyron and Len are no longer in college so this will not hurt your daughter in any way. I know that Shelby was innocently duped and am working to get to the bottom of this. I want to thank you for filling me in. What Shelby said has corroborated what I've been told by others so I think we're starting to really understand what happened."

Matt stood up and extended his hand to Buck. They shook hands as they walked to the door. Buck leaned close to Matt and whispered to him.

"I did a little research on you. Nice save of that girl in Europe. Shelby may be a little young for you, but you're the type of man I'd like her to find."

"Daddy!" Shelby screamed from behind. She had heard the whole thing. Matt was embarrassed even though he had done nothing wrong.

Matt spoke to Shelby.

"You are one of the most beautiful young women I have ever seen, but I don't think you have any problem finding guys who are interested in you. I am a few years too old for you, but I'm honored that your father would consider me worthy of your company."

That seemed to please everyone and Matt made his escape. As he walked to the car he laughed softly to himself. Too bad he didn't have a picture of Shelby and Buck. Imagine if Ced had been a witness to that!

CHAPTER ELEVEN

Monday morning brought forth a bright shiny day. Matt had returned home looking forward to the sunny weekend, which he enjoyed by running a 10K breast cancer awareness race. Matt wished he could be one of those people who loved to run, but if truth be told he hated running. He knew the exercise was good for him and he needed to keep in shape. He just wished he could find something that he loved, but until then he ran

Matt's normal pattern was to think as he ran. Matt thought about things he was working on. The running gave him a chance to reflect on where things stood and where they were going. Some of his best thinking on cases had come during long runs where he fell into a trancelike state that allowed him to open up his mind and really think.

Matt believed he had a good understanding of what had occurred with Coach Ken Reid in relation to Tyron and Len. He was very confident that he understood why Reid had Tyron and Len sign up for the correspondence course. He knew how the tutors were used and what Reid stood to gain if he kept the boys under his control. Matt thought that the NCAA Committee on Infractions would salivate to get Coach Reid in front of them to respond to charges that Reid used the correspondence course to blackmail the players in order to help his own career.

Where Matt kept having trouble was when he tried to figure out how it all fit within NCAA rules. It got a little tricky because a lot of what happened took place when Reid was a basketball coach at a junior college. The NCAA had no jurisdiction over junior colleges, but Matt thought he could make a case to show how the rules applied to Reid even as a junior college coach. Matt needed to figure out GCSU's role and responsibility in this and as far as Matt could tell, there was no proof that GCSU played any role or had any responsibility.

Unless someone could show that either Coach McEnroe or Coach Culp was involved with the correspondence course or at least knew about what

Reid was doing, Matt didn't see how GCSU could be charged. Matt had to help Lisa and her supervisors arrive at the same conclusion.

He thought about it as he ran. The race was in support of finding a cure for breast cancer. Matt had an aunt and a very close friend who had suffered with breast cancer so he donated to the cause and joined any efforts he could. Matt thought that cancer was the one disease that touched on all races, nationalities, sexes, ages, religions, etc. He enjoyed donating his time and efforts to a cause greater than himself.

As Matt ran past cheering observers, his mind raced through possible charges the NCAA could bring against GCSU. He had no idea what Lisa Lasham was thinking. In fact, he realized that Lisa didn't even know that Matt had spoken with the tutors. She had Tyron's interview, but she would need more than that. They would have to speak to Ken Reid at some point. Lisa didn't know Matt had documents that proved much of Tyron's story. He would have to share them with her at some point, but he was going to wait a bit longer to see where things fell. He would never withhold them from her, but he would wait until he saw what direction she was taking because he might be able to steer her towards a different path by giving her the documents at precisely the right moment.

That was one thing the general public and media failed to understand about the NCAA enforcement process. There was so much involved that related to timing. At times, the enforcement staff was backlogged on cases so they would take much more time in a current investigation. On the other side, if there were no cases waiting to be heard by the Committee on Infractions, the enforcement staff would, at times, rush a case to get it ready for the next hearing. Matt knew the juggling act the enforcement staff had to play so he kept up on the current caseload of the enforcement staff as best he could.

Matt returned to his office on Monday morning still contemplating what the NCAA may try to do. He called Ced, who had returned from California, and asked him to stop by the office. Matt was still thinking about the whole scenario when Ced walked in and plopped down on Matt's couch.

"What's up boss man?" Ced asked.

"Hey Ced, glad to have you back in town. What happened with Len? Did you ever find him?"

Ced stretched out relaxing. Matt was always amazed at how easily Ced could become comfortable just about anywhere.

"It's nice when things work out the way you want them to," Ced began. "I was able to locate Len, have a nice long discussion with him. During said discussion I persuaded him to stop acting like a fool. I helped him realize he has one of the all-time great mothers who just about tore her own heart out when she asked him to leave for the good of his younger siblings. I strongly persuaded him to get himself into rehab."

"So you got him to agree to go?" Matt wasn't really surprised. Ced could do just about anything he set his mind to, but this was pretty quick.

"He fought me for a while, but I convinced him that he had no choice. I think Len realized it was rehab or death. Initially Len agreed to go to a local facility in Southern California, but I, uhm let's just say, persuaded him to leave the state. I put him in a facility I know about in Orem, Utah."

Matt laughed. "Orem, Utah? How did you become familiar with a rehab facility in Orem, Utah?"

"When I was in the NBA I heard about this place. It is very quiet, but they work with celebrities and athletes and you never hear about them. I had a teammate who went there for a sex addiction and he said they changed his life. One time when we were in Salt Lake City to play the Jazz I went with him to see the place. He had a follow up meeting so I decided to see what it was like. They did great work and I became friends with one of the counselors."

"Ced, are you sure you weren't there for your own addictions?" Matt joked.

Ced looked hurt, but Matt knew he was just playing around. "Len balked at first, but I told him that Orem, Utah was quite a bit larger than the North Dakota town where he played basketball. I also told him that I knew the people and had teammates who went there. Once he heard NBA players had gone there he stopped fighting it."

"And do I dare ask how Len is paying for this rehab?"

"Wellllllllll, I have this friend who started a non-profit foundation to help with these types of situations. I was going to try to persuade my friend to sponsor Len and pay for his rehab." Ced looked at Matt with a big smile.

Matt couldn't even pretend to be angry.

"Ced, you have donated more than enough money to the foundation to have a say in this. If you believe we should use funds on Len Mallard I would never question you."

Ced smiled at Matt then said, "It's difficult to try to figure out which person to help because I know more needy people than you do. I don't want to be in the position of trying to figure out who needs the help the most. What I usually do is let you know when I run across someone and then trust you to make the right call. If you said no, I wouldn't ever hold it against you or our friendship."

Matt had started the foundation when the the owner of the European team gave him millions. Over the years, the Foundation had grown. Matt had donated the money to start up the foundation. Once word got out, Matt received donations from others. When people heard about it and heard some of the individual stories they couldn't wait to write a check. Ced had put in over a million dollars himself through the years.

"But Matt," Ced interrupted his thoughts. "I kind of promised Len Mallard's mama that I would try to help her boy so if the foundation didn't pay for it I guess I would."

"We can't let that happen," Matt responded. "Send me the bill and I'll make sure we cover it."

Matt was pleased that Ced had been able to locate Len Mallard and get him into a program. Mallard had received enough bad luck through the years and it was time for a little good luck, in the form of Ced Booker, to come his way.

"On to other business," Matt said. He then proceeded to explain where the investigation stood. He relayed his thoughts about whether or not GCSU was culpable for what Reid had done while employed by the junior college. Matt liked to confide in someone to get a second brain thinking about things. Matt trusted his own instinct, but it never hurt to bounce ideas off of someone else, someone he trusted and knew to be smart. Ced often played the role.

"It sounds like you are in a holding pattern until this NCAA chick decides her next move," Ced responded. "You have to talk to that loser Reid guy at some point, but I don't know what else you should do until then. How much do you know about Reid?"

Matt thought it over a minute. He knew some of Reid's background, but thought it might be a good time to see what Holly Cash could dig up with her computer skills.

He made a quick call to Holly asking her to go through her usual routine to find out anything and everything she thought might be pertinent.

"Do you have a birthdate for this Ken Reid? Or an address?"

Matt realized he had neither and told Holly.

"Is that going to be a problem?" Matt asked.

"Oh Matt, you are naïve when it comes to the cyberworld," Holly laughed. "I have a name and know two places he has worked so I'll be able to find him, but it would have been quicker and easier if you had anything else. Don't worry I'll get you what I can find."

They hung up the phone. Matt couldn't think of anything else to do except update GCSU's president on where things stood. He knew that President Scott would want to fire Ken Reid on the spot, but Matt would convince him to wait until the NCAA investigation was concluded. If GCSU did fire Reid, then Reid had no reason to cooperate or be interviewed. University presidents didn't like messy situations, especially if they could bring bad publicity down upon the university, but Matt would be able to convince President Scott to hold off on taking any action.

Matt and Ced went to get a bite to eat. As they departed from the restaurant Ced told Matt to call him if he needed him. Matt returned to his office still racking his brain trying to think of what else he could do. He called Holly again.

"Matt, I'm good, but I am working on other things and it has only been a couple of hours." Holly joked.

"No, that's not why I'm calling," Matt explained. "Do you think you could get the email string between Ken Reid and the other assistant coach, Randy Culp?"

"From what time period?" Holly asked.

"Ideally, it would be from the time frame beginning about four months before Ken Reid was hired at GCSU up to the present."

There was silence for a moment.

"Holly, are you still there?"

"Yes, I'm here," Holly stated. "I don't know what I could find. It would be fun to do it, but it would be a crime for me to hack into GCSU's computers to access Randy Culp's account. I can do it and don't even mind doing it, but thought you would want to know that you are asking me to commit a crime."

"What if I were able to get GCSU's president to give you permission?" Matt asked.

"Well, that would take some of the fun out of it, but that would probably be best for your peace of mind. Do me a favor though, tell him you just want permission and don't want anyone else. Ask him to leave the college's IT staff in the dark."

"Oh, you think there might be leaks? Someone in the IT staff might know Randy Culp?"

Holly laughed again. "No, I'm not worried about that, I just like a challenge and want to see if I can do it with no help from them and would like to see if I could go undetected by them. Tell the president that it will be an exercise to see how good their firewall is and I won't even charge them for it."

Matt didn't understand how Holly's mind worked, but she had proven herself far too many times for Matt to question her.

"Okay, let me get you permission and then go to work."

"Anything specific you are looking for?" Holly asked.

"Yes, very specific. I'm looking for any conversations the two of them had about Ken Reid being hired by GCSU, also any conversation that mentions Tyron Washington or Len Mallard."

"Tyron Washington and Len Mallard, got it," Holly stated.

"Yes, Tyron and Len are the unfortunate pawns in this whole thing and I'm hoping that we can get them some form of justice."

"Is there anything specific I'm looking for related to Tyron Washington and Len Mallard or do you want anything that even mentions them?"

"I'd like anything where their names are even part of the conversation, but I'm really looking for any discussion of a correspondence algebra course they took and received credit for while they were attending a junior college in North Dakota."

Matt had no qualms telling Holly everything he knew. He trusted her completely. Besides, he knew that she could find out anything she wanted to know about online. Her skills really scared Matt when he thought about how secure his information really was. Sometimes ignorance really is bliss!

They ended the phone call and Matt decided he had done all he could for the day. It might be a fruitless attempt, but Matt had such confidence in Holly he realized that he was expecting her to find results on this wild goose chase he had sent her on.

CHAPTER TWELVE

Holly was very good. She visited Matt the next morning handing him a manila envelope that was about two inches thick. She then went to Matt's refrigerator and pulled out a bottled water.

"Help yourself" Matt joked.

"I always do, but thanks for the invite though that takes the fun out of it!" Holly quipped.

"Explain that a little bit to me," Matt asked. "What is your need to sneak around going undetected instead of come in invited? Why do you get so much more joy out of the clandestine efforts?"

"Oh Matt, that is hard to try to explain to someone like you," Holly started. "You see, for computer hackers, we get a sense of joy and satisfaction knowing that we can do something, pitting our skills against those trying to stop us. The fun of the chase is more exciting then the actual work itself. You either are that way or you aren't and I can't really explain it. I get an even greater rush knowing that, as a woman, the computer industry thinks I can't do the same things the men can.

"Society thinks of us as criminals, but we don't see ourselves that way. Look at this current assignment. If I were just getting background on Ken Reid and searching for email discussions between him and the other coach, Randy Culp, it would have been very boring to me. But knowing that I was working around a secure system, trying to bypass their security, that made it fun and a challenge for me. Though I have to say that the system was ridiculously easy to hack into. For a university, the ease with which I got in was appalling."

"I might mention that to them when I'm through with this case," Matt stated. "Maybe I could give them your name as a consultant?"

Holly thought it over for a minute. "A university might be too mainstream for me, but if they would do it quietly with no public acknowledgement of my help, I might be willing to help them."

Matt had to laugh. If nothing else, Holly was consistent and very interesting. Who would think that a beautiful well-dressed woman like her, could hack into any computer system in the world? Well, maybe not any computer system, but Matt had yet to find a computer system that could stop her.

"I came upon something else that you may find interesting," Holly said to Matt and there was a twinkle in her eye as she spoke. "I didn't find any discussion between Reid and Culp about the correspondence course you mentioned, but I had a few spare moments so I researched the class itself. I included a description of the class, the outline students receive and then found a little nugget I thought you might find useful."

Matt could tell Holly was pleased with her efforts so he decided to let her continue, but instead Holly began walking towards the door.

"Wait, aren't you going to tell me what you found?" Matt asked.

"Oh, you'll see it soon enough. Call me if you have questions."

Holly scooted through the door before Matt could object. Now more curious than ever, Matt sat down to read the material Holly had delivered. The background on Ken Reid yielded little that Matt could use. Reid had a number of parking tickets as well as speeding violations. The police had been called out on domestic calls to Reid's home on multiple occasions so Matt understood Reid's ex-wife's hesitancy to talk. She was probably just happy to get him out of her life, but Matt was thankful she had sent him the material after the fact.

He turned to the email. Holly had included every email exchange between Reid and Randy Culp. There was quite a bit, Matt realized as he looked at the size of the stack of material. He settled in to read through it all, but discovered that Holly had saved him a huge chunk of time by including a sheet that directed Matt to the most relevant conversations, which she had highlighted to make it easier for him to find.

He read through the first few emails where Culp first brought up the possibility of Reid's employment. They were innocent enough. Culp told Reid that the other assistant coach had suddenly left and Coach McEnroe was trying to decide what to do with the open assistant position. They had several email exchanges between them that followed up with how it was to work with Coach McEnroe, what GCSU was like and other items that Reid had questions about.

So far there was nothing even approaching what could be argued was an NCAA violation. This exchange went back and forth over a period of one week then finally Matt saw something that caused him to pause.

Reid mentioned to Culp that he had two very good players and he thought he could help recruit them to GCSU if he were employed. That started down the path where one might start thinking GCSU offered the job to Reid if he brought the two players, but Matt continued reading and never found anything where there was clear and specific language saying that Reid would be hired on the condition of him being able to bring Tyron Washington and Len Mallard with him.

The first mention by Reid of the two players was a week before they signed up for the correspondence course. That proved nothing, but the timing was a big coincidence. Matt subscribed to the old line that one didn't believe in coincidences.

Matt knew, from past experience, that the NCAA Committee on Infractions didn't believe in coincidences either and they also didn't need absolute proof to convict someone. A "preponderance of the evidence" was their rule, or what a reasonable person might believe. Under that standard, Matt knew that Ken Reid would have been found guilty without the actual paper proof, but with the paperwork Reid had no out. Matt had to figure out how to best use that.

Matt found one interesting exchange where Culp asked how Reid knew he would be able to get the players to attend GCSU. Reid didn't say anything about the algebra course, but did say he could be very persuasive and had a strong influence on the two players.

Matt finished reading the material and sat back to think about it. There was nothing here that the NCAA could use against GCSU. Reid also never confirmed in an email anything about the algebra course so nobody could conclude from the emails that Culp had any knowledge of what Reid had done.

Matt finally got to the last group of papers Holly had provided. It started with an email exchange between Ken Reid and a teacher at the junior college who happened to be the head of the math department. In the email, Reid mentioned that Tryon Washington and Len Mallard were taking a correspondence course and would need a proctor for the final exam. The teacher, Josh Mayberry, had responded saying he would be happy to proctor the exam in exchange for a few beers. It was obvious that Mayberry and Reid were good friends.

Reid had responded to Mayberry by saying he would bring over a couple of six-packs and they could watch whatever game was on that week while the players took the final. Mayberry had agreed telling Reid to "not bring the cheap stuff".

Matt decided he might need to visit with Josh Mayberry. He realized he was still in pause mode in the investigation and didn't like the fact that he was waiting on Lisa Lasham at the NCAA to make the next move. He decided to try to push her a little so he picked up the phone and dialed her number.

She picked up on the first ring. "NCAA enforcement, Lisa Lasham speaking."

"Hello Miss Lasham, this is Matt Colter. I thought I'd touch base to see where we stood."

"Oh, hello Mr. Colter." Matt could hear the disappointment in her voice. "As you know, I'm not just working on one case. I've had to set the GCSU matter aside for a little bit to work on some other matters that are more pressing. I'll get back to you in the next week or two, have a nice day!"

Matt heard the click on the other end. He was annoyed, but refused to get angry. This was one of the things that really bothered him about working with the NCAA enforcement staff. When they wanted something, they wanted it immediately. Then they would set it aside for weeks on end making one wonder why there was such a rush to get it in the first place. Schools and lawyers were forced to work on the NCAA enforcement staff member's schedule, waiting for them to have time to move the case along.

Matt decided to use his knowledge of how the enforcement staff worked as well as his connections at the NCAA. He called his old boss, Ed Raines, who just happened to be Lisa's current boss.

Ed didn't answer on the first ring. Matt got his voice mail and decided to leave a message.

"Hello Ed, hope you are doing well. This is Matt Colter and I wondered if you had a couple of moments to discuss something with me. No hurry, but if you get a second I'd appreciate it if you could call. Thanks."

Matt hung up the phone. He knew that Lisa would be royally pissed off at Matt going above her, but Matt didn't care. In fact, he would enjoy it immensely if this all worked out in his favor.

Matt didn't have much time to contemplate it because Ed Raines called him back in fifteen minutes. They caught up on old times then Ed asked what he could do for Matt.

"Listen Ed, I know you supervise Lisa Lasham. She is quite a pistol by the way, lots of energy and enthusiasm for the job."

Matt would never tell Ed that he thought Lisa was a little immature and needed some additional supervisory help. He didn't want to put Ed on the defensive. If he was going to get what he wanted, Matt knew that a little flattery wouldn't hurt.

"Yes, Lisa is one of our up and comers. She has shown a real skill set for this work," Ed replied.

Matt liked Ed very much, but he knew that Ed was a true believer in the NCAA enforcement mission and didn't take criticism of the enforcement staff or any of its members well. Matt would have liked to be completely honest with Ed because he liked working for Ed and thought Ed did a great job, but Matt knew that Ed had one real blind spot about critically looking at the enforcement staff and admitting that there were some staff members who probably didn't belong.

"Lisa and I were just talking about the GCSU matter. I told her that GCSU's president was very involved and wanted to see movement, but Lisa explained to me that she was very busy and had to put this aside for a bit. I understand that completely, but the president of GCSU doesn't have experience in NCAA enforcement matters and he is anxious to see progress."

"You say that GCSU's president asked you to call?"

"No, not directly," Matt responded. He knew that Ed would take it very seriously if a university president wondered why there was a delay. Matt thought that was the best approach, rather than putting his own views against Lisa's. "The president asked me to keep him very closely updated and since there hasn't been anything new for a little while he is getting restless."

"Thanks for calling me Matt," Ed responded. "Let me talk to Lisa and see if I can help free up her schedule. We'll get back to you."

Matt thanked Ed for taking the concerns seriously, though Matt knew he would. In fact, Matt felt a little guilty about using Ed this way, but having worked with the enforcement staff and now on the other side, the guilt didn't last long. Matt had learned that you couldn't bully the staff, but you could find other ways to get what you were looking for.

Sure enough, Lisa called him shortly thereafter.

"Mr. Colter," Lisa began. "It seems as if Ed Raines has decided that we should move a little more quickly on the GCSU case."

"Oh really? What made him decide that?" Matt asked innocently.

"I'm not really sure, but he asked me to get back on it this week so I'm letting you know that I'm going back on campus to interview Ken Reid and perhaps a couple of other people. If you'd like to be there contact Shawn Morgan and he can get you the times and location. The first interview is Thursday morning at 10 a.m."

Matt hung up the phone and wondered why he felt such immense satisfaction. He basked in the feeling for just a moment then made his travel arrangements back to GCSU with a quick trip to see Josh Mayberry first. Knowing how the NCAA works had served Matt well in the past and head just done so again!

CHAPTER THIRTEEN

It seemed as if Matt spent a good chunk of his life on planes. It was funny, but he had one time thought seriously about not playing basketball because he disliked flying so much. He had grown used to the flying, but now got very annoyed by the things he saw while flying. It seemed as if people got dumber the minute they walked into the airport.

One time Matt had seen a person open up the overhead bin to get something. A bag had fallen and hit the passenger sitting below the bin in the head. The flight had been delayed while a doctor looked at the cut that had been opened in the woman's head. The flight attendants had to fill out paperwork and have the people involved sign it, probably to protect the airline from a lawsuit. Finally everything had been resolved and they were ready to back away from the gate, a half hour late. A person stood up, opened up the same bin, and another bag had fallen on the same person. Matt recalled that he had said very loudly, "Did you not just see what happened? Did you not understand that we've been delayed because of a bag falling on that woman?"

The poor man who had opened up the bin the second time apologized profusely to the entire cabin and quietly sat back down. He had never looked at Matt during the flight and quickly exited the plane upon landing. Matt had felt badly, but couldn't believe the man had opened the bin after all that had ensued.

Matt had promised himself that he would stay calm during flights, but he could write a book about the stupidity he had witnessed while flying! It never ceased to amaze him.

Matt had been able to contact Josh Mayberry by phone. Mayberry had been troubled that Matt wouldn't give him more information over the phone, but he agreed to meet at 7:00 a.m. Wednesday morning. Matt had rushed to the airport to make a late flight on Tuesday evening arriving around midnight to his hotel. He would talk with Mayberry then catch another flight to be on GCSU's campus the following morning. Ah, the glamorous life of an investigating attorney!

With about five hours of sleep, Matt hurried over to Mayberry's office. It was a small corner office at the junior college. It was a shame that junior colleges were so cash strapped because they did a lot of good work and saved people money before moving onto a four-year school to complete a degree.

Matt knocked on the open door and entered. He was greeted by a man who looked like he could be a student. Matt was often told that he looked young, but this guy looked like he was a decade younger than Matt. The man stood up to greet him.

"Hi, Josh Mayberry and before you say anything, yes I'm old enough to be teaching here." Mayberry grinned as he extended his hand toward Matt. "I'm often told that I look like I could be a student, but I'm actually 30 years old."

Matt wasn't going to say he had been thinking that exact thing. He handed Mayberry his business card and thanked him for agreeing to talk as he sat down.

"I've been hired by GCSU to assist them with an NCAA matter they are dealing with." Matt began.

"GCSU? That's where our old basketball coach works. Do you know Ken Reid?" Mayberry asked.

"I haven't met him yet, but I will soon," Matt responded. "The NCAA matter involves the men's basketball program so I'm sure Ken Reid will be interviewed at some point."

"That's exciting!"

Matt couldn't get over the fact that Josh Mayberry was 30 years old. The excitement on his face made him look 18.

"Exciting isn't the word I would use," Matt stated. "NCAA investigations are often long and tedious and never fun for those involved, but they are necessary."

"So what does any of that have to do with me?" Mayberry questioned.

"Well, during the investigation the names of two players have surfaced who attended school here."

"Tyron Washington and Len Mallard," Mayberry quickly stated.

"Yes, that is correct," Matt answered. "Do you know them?"

"Not personally, but I am a big fan of basketball and go to all of the games here. They were both great players for us and I knew they had followed their coach to GCSU. I followed their careers at GCSU and know they did pretty well there. Ken Reid is a great coach and he helped them tremendously."

Matt found it interesting to see how highly Mayberry thought of Ken Reid. This was the first person who had spoken well of Reid. Matt couldn't figure out if Mayberry was also a pawn in this matter or if he had been acting in concert with Reid. How exactly should he get to the point?

"Did you ever teach or work with Tyron or Len while they were here?" Matt asked.

"No, I never had the good fortune to teach them. I never even met either one of them and only saw them a few times around campus. Of course I saw them regularly at the games they played in."

"So you never were involved with them in any way academically?" Matt queried.

"No, not in any way."

"Are you sure about that? You never had any academic involvement with them? Never helped them with any academic work, never substituted in a class they were in?"

Mayberry snorted in disdain. "We don't substitute for other teachers here. This isn't a high school. You may look down on junior colleges, but we are just like any other institution of higher learning."

Matt had hit a nerve without intending to do so. "I wasn't trying to look down on junior colleges. I value the work that is done here and across the nation. I just am not real clear on how things work and wanted to make one hundred percent sure that you had never had any involvement of any type with Tyron Washington or Len Mallard academically."

"Well you can now be one hundred percent clear," Mayberry said.

"So you only saw them as a fan of the basketball team, never saw them in any type of academic setting?"

"Mr. Colter," Mayberry was trying to control his anger. "I've told you as clearly as I can be that I had no academic involvement with either of those young men. I don't know how much clearer I can say that to you. If you have nothing else I need to get prepared for my class."

Matt reached into his briefcase and pulled out the final exams of Washington and Mallard.

"Mr. Mayberry, have you seen these exams before?"

Mayberry took the exams and looked at them.

"These are not my exams. They look like exams the young men took at another institution."

Mayberry seemed very pleased with himself. He was sure that Matt Colter had no idea what he was doing and had screwed things up.

"Could you look at the bottom of the last page?" Matt asked.

Mayberry turned through the pages coming to last one. Matt watched his eyes as he slowly scanned down the page. When he got to the last part his eyes just about popped out of his head.

"Could you tell me what you see at the bottom of the page?"

"Yes, I see what you are getting at. This says I proctored the final exam and has my signature, but I never did any such thing."

"Are you sure about that?" Matt asked. "Do you remember Coach Reid coming over with a couple of six-packs of beer and watching a game with you while the two young men took their final exam?"

Matt watched Mayberry's face. He saw defeat in his eyes.

"How did you know about the six-packs of beer? Did one of those players tell you that? It just isn't true!"

But Matt could see that it was true. He could see that Mayberry realized he was in some trouble. He decided to push a little.

"I'm not going to tell you how I came to know what happened. I'm not sure what I'm going to do with this, but you can tell me anything else you have to say that you think might be helpful to both of us and then I'll be on my way."

"I have nothing else to say. It is my word against those players and I think a faculty member's word will mean more than a couple of dumb jocks!"

Matt took the exam back and put it in his briefcase. He wasn't going to get anything more here. As he stood to go he had to make one final point.

"You have said you are like any other institution of higher learning. I don't think those institutions would allow a teacher to proctor an exam while drinking beer and watching a basketball game. And before you get too far along the path of your word versus two... what did you call them, oh yes dumb jocks. Before you go too far down that path, you have to be very sure that there was no email exchange between you and Coach Reid discussing the arrangements."

Matt walked out leaving Mayberry sitting in stunned silence. He knew that would create some doubt in Mayberry's mind. Matt went out the front door and had to cross right below Mayberry's office window as he went to his car. The window was opened just a crack and Matt heard Mayberry's frantic voice.

"Listen Ken, he knows all about the correspondence course. He has the final exams and may have something where we discussed it in an email. He knows about us watching the game and drinking beer while they did the exams. You have to do something about this."

Matt sat there listening. After a few moments of silence where it was clear that Mayberry was listening to Ken Reid speaking, Mayberry spoke again.

"Yes, that is good. Make sure they beat the crap out of him before he goes into your interview. He keeps the final exam in his briefcase. I don't know what else he has, but if you take his briefcase you can find out for yourself."

Now Matt had a physical threat to worry about. He was heading back to GCSU to interview Ken Reid tomorrow morning at 10:00 a.m. If Reid was planning on doing anything to Matt it would have to be before then. Matt had a contingency plan in place for these types of emergencies.

He got in his car and made a couple of phone calls. Perhaps nothing would come of this, but just like the boy scouts, he had to always be prepared!

CHAPTER FOURTEEN

Upon his arrival at the airport near GCSU's campus, Matt pulled out his cell phone and made a call. He checked to make sure everything was in place before leaving the airport. If Ken Reid was planning an attack on Matt, it would have to come right now on his way to the hotel or tomorrow morning before he arrived for the interviews at GCSU. Those were the times Matt was most vulnerable.

Secure that his arrangements were all in place, Matt picked up his rental car and drove to his hotel. Matt had never been trained in counter-surveillance techniques, but he knew enough to keep a constant eye in his rearview mirror. He made sudden turns at familiar areas to see if anyone followed. He was pretty sure that nobody tracked him from the airport, which didn't surprise him.

Matt didn't think that Ken Reid had shown anything that would lead Matt to believe this would be a well-organized attack. Matt was pretty sure that Reid would come straight at him in an awkward attempt to intimidate him.

Matt stopped at a drive-thru sandwich shop on his way to the hotel. He wouldn't go out that evening to eliminate any chance of being surprised. After getting his food he drove straight to the hotel, parking under a very well lit area in full view of the front of the hotel.

Matt checked in and went straight to his room. He read through the material in preparation for tomorrow's interview. There wasn't much on television, but Matt always brought something to read, this time on his I-pad. He loved his I-pad because he could carry it instead of four or five books.

At around 8:00 p.m. there was a knock on his hotel room door. He looked though the peephole, but saw only darkness.

"Yes, can I help you?" Matt asked through the closed door.

"Yes sir, hotel security, we've had a report of some trouble on this floor. Could we talk with you for a few minutes?"

This was the feeble attempt Matt was expecting.

"Can you give me a few minutes? I'll be right with you," Matt responded.

Matt quickly pushed a button on his phone signaling to put his plan in motion. He had to stall for a bit.

"Can you please give me your name?" Matt asked through the door.

"Uh…….yes sir. My name is Rick and I'm head of security here."

"Ok, thanks Rick. I'll be right with you."

Matt called the hotel front desk and asked for the manager. He explained that a man was at his door saying he was head of security and that his name was Rick. The manager told Matt that there was no head of security for the hotel and nobody named Rick worked there. He told Matt he would call the police.

Matt went back to the door and could still see nothing through the peephole. He decided to just wait and not say anything.

The man knocked again. "Sir, are you okay? I really just need a minute of your time."

"I'm fine, I just am finishing up on a phone call, I'll be right with you."

Matt was trying to stall for as long as he could. He heard a noise in the hallway and looked again through the peephole. Now he could see light. Upon a more careful look Matt realized he could see the hallway and the doors across the hall. He waited another minute then made another call.

"It appears as if he got spooked and left," Matt stated. "I'm going to stay in my room, but check the hallway. Be careful to not run into the police. The hotel manager said he was going to call them."

Matt sat back down thinking things through. This was the type of thing Matt thought that Ken Reid might do. He didn't appear to be the most intelligent person Matt had come across. There would definitely be another opportunity tomorrow morning.

Matt pulled up GCSU's website on his computer and accessed the men's basketball page. Looking at Ken Reid's photo, Matt saw that Reid was 5'10" and weighed 220 pounds. Matt wasn't worried about Reid, but didn't want to underestimate Reid's friends, whoever they may be.

The following morning Matt prepared to leave. He had not been bothered any more during the evening. As he packed his briefcase he made sure he had everything he would need. Matt made a call on his phone to signal that he was leaving. He carefully eased his way into the hallway, checking both ways to see if anyone was waiting for him.

It was no surprise that Ken Reid had been able to locate his hotel room. There were only a couple of decent hotels within 20 miles of GCSU's campus. Getting his actual room number would have been more difficult, but Matt thought that in a small town, one would have friends working everywhere so it wasn't unreasonable to think that Reid had friends who could find out that information.

Matt walked quickly to his car and got in. He backed out of his parking space half expecting someone to be standing there trying to block him, but nobody was. Matt had to admit, his adrenaline was pumping. He wasn't that worried about physically being hurt, but any type of physical threat got him thinking back to helping the owner's son in Europe. Matt knew he could take care of himself, but in this day and age, one always had to worry about weapons.

Again, Matt watched his rearview mirror as he drove. He picked up on a white Chevy pick-up truck that appeared to be following him. Matt made a couple of unnecessary turns to make sure he wasn't imagining anything. The Chevy made the same turns and was careful to keep four or five cars behind. Matt picked up speed just a little and the Chevy did the same. Matt slowed down at a spot where it was unnecessary and the Chevy slowed as well.

Sure that he was being followed, Matt picked up his cell phone and made a call. He spoke slowly describing the vehicle. He thought he had seen three people inside the truck, but hadn't had a clear view to be sure. Matt hung up the phone and finished his drive to GCSU. The athletics department was set off from the rest of the campus so Matt drove into a parking lot that only had about ten cars in it. The parking lot was big, probably for parking on game days, but it appeared that the day to day use was minimal.

Matt drove to an open area away from the other cars and parked his car. He sat for minute looking into his mirror. The Chevy had pulled into the parking lot, but was sitting about 30 yards away. Another car pulled in from another direction and also sat idling. Matt had to trust his plan so he gathered his things exiting the car. The Chevy raced towards him pulling within ten feet and screeching to a stop. The other car quietly pulled around behind the Chevy.

Three men exited the Chevy walking towards Matt. The biggest of the three spoke.

"We don't want to hurt you. Give us your wallet and briefcase and throw your car keys as far as you can and we'll leave without touching you."

Matt was surprised by their direct approach. He had thought they would attempt to hit him then take his things, but they were the talking type. Matt turned to face them squarely.

"I'm afraid I can't do that. I need my briefcase for a meeting I'm going to and I'm sure I'll need my wallet later today. I also will need my driver's license in order to get on a plane to go back home."

The smaller, nastier looking of the three stepped forward. He wore dirty jeans, a plaid shirt and a small stocking cap. He hadn't shaved in a couple of days.

"Listen moron, my friend here offered you a chance to escape without getting hurt. For me, I'd just as soon put a beating on you!"

He glared at Matt, just waiting for the opportunity to pounce.

Matt continued to act calm, but his heart was beating quickly. The door to the second car opened quietly and Matt saw what he needed to see.

"I don't think three on one is very fair," Matt stated. "I'm not much of a fighter, but I really did mean it when I said I needed my wallet and briefcase. I'm willing to just forget all about this and have us all be on our way."

The smaller man laughed. "Of course you don't think three on one is fair because you are the one. Now either give us what we've asked for or face the odds!"

"I thought it would only be fair if I evened up the odds a little bit."

"How are you going to do that? Are you going to split into two?" The man laughed and looked at his companions while threatening Matt.

A deep voice boomed from behind the three men. "No, he doesn't have to split into two. Me and my friend here will even things up three on three."

The men jumped upon hearing the voice then turned all shades of white when they spun around to see Ced Booker and one of Ced's friends calmly standing behind them. Ced was imposing enough with his size and strength, but his friend looked like he had been chiseled out of granite. His arms were bigger than Ced's and he wore a tank top that revealed them.

The three men stood dumbstruck for a minute.

"Gentlemen, my offer still stands," Matt said. "I can forget all about this if you want to just be on your way."

"Ssssure, we appreciate that mister. We'll just be on our way," the first man said.

"Just a minute," Ced interrupted. "I'm not quite as forgiving as my friend here. I'll let you go like he said, but on one condition."

The three men looked terrified. Matt almost felt sorry for them, but he knew what they would have done if the roles were reversed so he couldn't feel too badly for them.

"Anything, just tell us what you want and we'll give it to you. Do you want our wallets? Our cell phones? What do you want?"

Ced snarled in a deep menacing voice, "Tell us who put you up to this."

The first man tried to be brave and stated "nobody put us up to it. We just saw what we thought were easy pickings, but now we see we were mistaken."

"NOT GOOD ENOUGH!" Ced bellowed as he moved towards the men.

The big man caved. He wanted no part of Ced or Ced's large companion. The man explained that his good friend Ken Reid had asked them to get Matt's briefcase. They were told to not hurt Matt in any way, just take the briefcase and run.

Good to their word, Matt and Ced let the men leave. Matt wasn't worried about running into them in the future. He figured the sight of Ced and his friend were more than enough to dissuade them from having further involvement.

"Thanks for having my back," Matt shook hands with the two men.

"No problem," Ced responded. "That little guy looked like he may have bitten your leg if we hadn't been here. You might have been able to take the other two, but that little guy would have taken you down!"

Matt laughed and thanked them again. There would be a small bonus in Ced's pay. This wasn't part of his job, but Matt knew he could count on Ced and not only count on him, Ced would enjoy this aspect of the work.

"By the way, who is your friend here? He almost made the big guy wet his pants just by looking at him!"

"Oh sorry, Matt meet Larry Smith. Larry is a competitive bodybuilder and a long time friend of mine."

Matt shook hands and said, "Thanks for the assist. You two go have some lunch on me. And Larry, if I can ever return the favor all you have to do is ask. Thanks again."

Matt got back in the car and drove to the GCSU campus. He now had to figure out how to play the Ken Reid interview. Should he confront Reid with the information he had during the interview or maybe immediately afterwards. After thinking it over a bit Matt did what he usually did. He planned on being a straight shooter and letting the chips fall where they may. He hoped some might fall on Ken Reid.

CHAPTER FIFTEEN

Matt had scheduled a meeting with President Scott and the AD Mike Love before Ken Reid's interview. He needed to share the progress in the investigation and get some marching orders going forward.

Matt was ushered into President Scott's office. Mike Love was already there looking a bit nervous. Matt hadn't seen Mike Love nervous before and wondered if there was some contention between President Scott and Love. President Scott stood up to shake Matt's hand.

"Mr. Colter, nice to see you again. Let's get right to it, what have you learned and what counsel do you have for us? Is GCSU going to go before the NCAA Committee on Infractions?"

So that must have been some of the discussion before he arrived. Surely Mike Love hadn't told President Scott that this was nothing only to learn that it was bigger than he had thought? Maybe that was the reason he was acting nervous?

"This is an interesting issue if you like to delve into NCAA language and jurisdiction issues. But not so interesting if you are the school in the middle of this."

"That doesn't sound good," President Scott interrupted. "It sounds like we have some issues?"

"Yes there are some issues," Matt responded. "Here is what I've found so far."

Matt spent the next half hour explaining the circumstances surrounding the correspondence course and Ken Reid's involvement with it and the two players Tyron Washington and Len Mallard. Matt pulled out the documentation that proved Reid had done this intentionally. He showed them the work the tutors had done and explained how Reid had misled the tutors into helping the two young men cheat.

"That sounds like we have enough to fire Ken Reid right now," President Scott stated.

"That is a decision for you to make, but you need to consider this investigation and what effect Ken Reid's firing might have upon it," Matt reminded them. "We are going to interview Ken Reid shortly, I'm hoping that we might get him to answer the question about whether or not anyone at GCSU knew about this or found out about it after the fact."

Mike Love spoke up for the first time. "Are you saying that if nobody at GCSU knew about what Reid did at the junior college, we are off the hook with the NCAA?"

Matt looked at Love and could see the hope in his eyes. He hadn't realized that Love might be in some trouble with the administration. But then again, Love was the one who pushed to hire Ned McEnroe as the head coach. A small school like GCSU wasn't used to being in the limelight for the wrong reasons. This was a proud academic institution. Matt imagined that many of the faculty didn't like seeing the university's name in the paper for all of the wrong reasons. They ventured for the first time into big time college athletics and it looked like it was going to bite them.

Matt had to be careful how he answered. "That is the interesting NCAA jurisdiction issue I've been contemplating. If Ken Reid committed some type of academic fraud before he arrived at GCSU and nobody from GCSU was involved, then it would seem that the NCAA couldn't bring charges against the school."

"Well that's great news!" Love exclaimed.

"Perhaps," Matt began. "But we aren't sure whether or not anyone at GCSU knew about it. You also have to consider that once GCSU hired Ken Reid, now you have an employee of GCSU who knew about the academic fraud and didn't report it as NCAA rules require. That permitted Tyron Washington and Len Mallard to compete as student-athletes at GCSU when they were not academically eligible. Is the school liable for that?"

"No!," Love shouted. "How can we be responsible for something we didn't know, was happening. We wouldn't have allowed them to play had we known what had happened. Ken Reid might have cheated, but we didn't know that when we hired him."

"Mike," President Scott responded. "Based on the evidence we've seen, I don't think there is any way you can say Ken Reid MIGHT have cheated. He definitely did cheat. We benefitted from that cheating. There are no two ways about it. We should have been more careful when we approved Reid's hiring. We are responsible for that."

Matt liked President Scott even more. It appeared he was ready to admit the mistakes and take whatever punishment the NCAA meted out.

"There's another aspect of this that I would like to discuss with you," Matt started. "This is something I haven't really faced before and I know what I would do, but I reminded myself last night that I am working for you and I need to talk this through with you."

"Go ahead and tell us about it," President Scott said.

"I'm working with a young woman from the NCAA on this case. Or I guess I should say I'm trying to work with her. She isn't one who likes to share her thoughts or to discuss the aspects of the case. We reached a point early on where she attempted to contact your former players Tyron Washington and Len Mallard and failed. She told me that she was thinking of just bringing allegations against GCSU for working out a deal to hire Ken Reid, but only if he brought two players with him."

"It is my understanding that nobody actually said that," Mike Love blurted out.

Matt knew that Love had been briefed on the case. He thought the compliance director Shawn Morgan might have been keeping his boss informed. Matt wouldn't have faulted Shawn for doing that, but now it seemed based on some of Love's comments, that he was getting information from one of the coaches. It had to be either Ned McEnroe or perhaps Randy Culp. Matt thought that Culp would know more about campus politics and how to play that game than McEnroe. Matt had to be careful what he said in front of Love.

"You are right, nobody has come right out and confirmed that there was a deal in place. I don't think the NCAA could prove that and I believe the investigator was bluffing. But you hired me to get the truth, no matter where it led, so I was able to find and contact Tyron Washington overseas. He told us the story about the correspondence class. I then found others who confirmed it, including the tutors and I received the paperwork I showed you. We also located Len Mallard."

Matt looked from Scott to Love. Scott's face was calm, but Love was visibly irritated. Love spoke.

"You mean to say that the NCAA had nothing, but you dug up the proof against us? Aren't you our lawyer? Aren't you supposed to be helping us?"

Matt waited for Love to calm down. These were the types of questions that helped Matt decide for whom he did and didn't want to work. Matt could tell that Mike Love was quickly falling into the latter category, but he thought President Scott had more substance to him. He would find out depending upon what Scott said right now.

As if on cue, President Scott began speaking very evenly and without emotion. "Mike, I hired Mr. Colter to uncover the truth and that is what I expect him to do. I don't want him to just think about helping us avoid NCAA sanctions. I want to find out what happened and rectify the problem, if there is a problem. Mr. Colter knows that he needs to go further than the NCAA might if he thinks that is necessary."

Again, Matt liked hearing what President Scott had to say. He was a real leader and those were the type of people with whom Matt liked to work. He could tell that Mike Love didn't agree, but wouldn't say anything that might get him in hot water with his own president.

Matt pushed this advantage. "That brings me to the next point. The NCAA knows about the correspondence course, but has no proof other than what Tyron Washington told us in an interview. The NCAA investigator decided to not pursue getting the proof. She took Washington at his word. She doesn't know about my conversations with the tutors nor about the paperwork showing the work the tutors did. She also doesn't know about my conversation with Josh Mayberry, the head of the math department who proctored the final exam in the correspondence course, if you can call it that."

"Why are you telling us this?" Mike Love asked.

"I realized that you are obligated by NCAA rules to report violations of those rules as you become aware of them. Bylaw 10 is the ethical conduct bylaw in the NCAA manual. As an employee of an NCAA school, you have the obligation to provide the NCAA information if you know about NCAA violations. I am not governed by the NCAA. I want to give you the information and let you decide what to do with it."

President Scott thought about it. Matt could tell he was mulling something over so he waited. Finally Scott said, "Well Mike, I guess we have to decide what to give the NCAA. They got the information about the correspondence course from the attorney we hired. Is that enough or should we provide the proof as well? Isn't that what you are asking Mr. Colter? I gather you think the NCAA hasn't followed up like it should so you are wondering if a school has the obligation to hang itself if the NCAA isn't going far enough?"

Matt was very pleased. President Scott was a very intelligent man and had grasped Matt's question completely. Telling the NCAA that a violation was committed was one thing, but providing the proof that they would not have found made even Matt question how far did one need to go to self-incriminate?

Rather than just provide an answer, President Scott had asked Mike Love what he thought. Matt was pretty sure that President Scott was testing Mike Love to see what type of athletic director he had. Mike Love better be careful how he answered, but Matt had the feeling that Mike Love had already exposed himself. He confirmed it when he finally responded.

"I am all for being honest and playing by the rules." Love started. "Mr. Colter has provided the information that will explain what happened. He has also said that there is no proof that anyone from GCSU was involved. I think we should inform the NCAA about that, but I don't believe we have any obligation to furnish them with the actual proof. If the NCAA isn't going to do a thorough investigation then we shouldn't be paying to have someone do it for them. If I did my job like that, I'm sure I wouldn't be employed long. That is why I excel in my job."

Matt was watching President Scott's face as Mike Love spoke. President Scott didn't show much emotion, but Matt could tell that Mike Love had just sealed his own fate.

"Thanks Mike, that gives me a lot to think about." President Scott stated.

Mike Love got up as if to leave. "If that is it, I have a meeting I'm late for and I need to see about a couple of other things as well." Love rushed out of the room.

Matt still hadn't really gotten an answer to his question. Did GCSU want Matt to provide everything to the NCAA?

"Mr. Colter, if you have a minute can you sit back down?" President Scott asked.

Matt sat back down.

"Being a college president is a tough job, with so many different areas pulling on you. I have trusted myself to hire good people and let them do their job. When I see that I've made a mistake I don't wait to fix it." President Scott looked at his hands as he spoke.

"I see that I've made a few mistakes in athletics. I will let Ken Reid be interviewed, but then I'm going to terminate his contract later this week. I hope that won't cause problems for your investigation."

Matt shook his head and said he didn't think it would be a problem. President Scott wasn't finished.

"You interviewed the other assistant coach, Randy Culp? What did you think of him?"

Matt thought about it for a moment. This was outside the attorney/client agreement, but Matt had never shied away from sharing his opinions when asked.

"I don't know if we will ever find any proof that Randy Culp committed any violations. If you are looking to take action against him, I don't think you can do based on his committing an NCAA violation."

"That's not what I asked you," President Scott smiled. "I've been impressed with how you handle yourself. I want to hear what your impression of Randy Culp is."

Matt smiled back. "I was getting to that. I don't think he can be terminated based on committing an NCAA violation, but I would have never hired him in the first place. I would never allow my child to come play for a program where he was coaching. Not speaking as an attorney, but as a former player, I don't get much of a sense that he has a great basketball IQ. I think he is better suited to politics."

"That was the honest appraisal I was searching for from you," President Scott laughed. "Our contracts with assistant coaches are for one year. I'm going to let Ned McEnroe know that both of his assistants' contracts will not be renewed. I'm also going to think about what penalties we can self-impose. I understand that you might find a way to convince the NCAA that we aren't responsible the violations and I hope you do that, but I'm still going to take some steps to fix what is clearly broken."

President Scott stood to indicate that Matt's time was concluded. They shook hands and agreed to keep the communication lines open. President

Scott told Matt that he should report directly to him and not to Mike Love. Matt picked up his things and started to leave.

"One last thing Mr. Colter," President Scott called after Matt. "Provide everything you have to the NCAA. We are going to cooperate completely with their investigation, but please keep records of what you found and what they wouldn't have found without your help. We may be able to use that in our defense."

Matt smiled as he left. President Scott was a lot more savvy than Matt had believed. This could get interesting!

CHAPTER SIXTEEN

Matt walked into the designated interview room. Lisa Lasham was sitting at the table with her notebooks and recorder spread out over the table. She glanced up when Matt walked in.

"Oh, hello Mr. Colter."

"Hello Miss Lasham, how are things at the NCAA?"

"Things are fine as always," Lisa stated.

Matt had to decide when to share information with Lisa. He could start right now, but didn't think he'd have time before Ken Reid came in. Instead he decided to mention it to her.

"I wanted to let you know I've discovered quite a bit of information I'll share with you after we conclude with Ken Reid's interview. A lot of this has come in very recently so I haven't had time to get you up to speed, but I may jump in with some information during this interview and I didn't want you to be surprised."

"Mr. Colter, you know the obligations of NCAA member institutions to share information with the NCAA enforcement staff."

"Miss Lasham, you don't need to start explaining NCAA rules to me. I know them and worked in them long before you joined the esteemed organization. I have some information I'll share, information I might remind you, that you had decided to not pursue. So don't start the sanctimonious act with me."

Lisa was definitely angry. Her cheeks turned bright red, but before she could respond Shawn Morgan walked into the room followed by Ken Reid.

"Hello everyone," Shawn greeted them. "This is Coach Ken Reid."

Lisa stood to introduce herself, Matt followed suit. Lisa indicated the chair that Coach Reid should sit in. She began going through her regular routine of explaining the purpose of the interview, having Reid sign various forms and then asking for permission to record the interview.

Matt watched Coach Reid. This was the man that arranged for three men to either attack him or at the very least to steal his briefcase. Part of Matt wanted to jump across the table to throttle the man, but Matt had always been able to control his emotions. He wanted to see how Reid reacted when he saw Matt. By now, he would have heard that the attempt had failed and would have known he was doomed. Matt saw very little nervousness while he watched Reid. Maybe he had accepted his fate.

Lisa began her questioning. She began by circling around the subject of how Reid had been hired at GCSU. She didn't want to come right out and ask him if it had been a package deal for him to be hired upon the condition of him delivering two players, but she couldn't seem to get Reid to even begin approaching that subject.

Matt was always fascinated by the NCAA approach. The investigators were taught to begin the interview by asking the interviewee basic simple questions to form a bond and to get the interviewee accustomed to answering questions. The NCAA staff would then start zeroing in with the questions before targeting the actual issue they were there to discuss. The hope was that the interviewee would get comfortable with the give and take and just begin talking about a subject without the need for the interviewer to ask point blank questions directly related to the issue at hand. Matt had seen this technique work numerous times, but it wasn't a technique he liked. It seemed to take forever, making hour long interviews last two to three hours.

Ken Reid deftly avoided saying anything of substance. Finally Lisa saw that she would have to be more direct. She asked matter of factly whether or not GCSU discussed Tyron Washington and Len Mallard during his hiring process.

"Of course the coaches here knew I had a couple of very good players," Reid stated. "They knew that, as a very good coach, I would have influence with the two players when they chose where to continue their education, but nobody at GCSU ever told me that my hiring was conditional upon bringing those players with me."

Well that was very direct. Matt was surprised that Ken Reid was acting a little cocky. Surely he knew that his attempt to get Matt's material had failed. Then it dawned on Matt that perhaps the three men hadn't contacted Reid. Matt hadn't put his material on the table like Lisa had. He had stowed his briefcase under his seat, out of the view of Reid. Could Reid really think that

Matt had no other proof of what Reid had done at the junior college? This might get interesting.

Lisa continued questioning Reid. She finally got around to asking about the correspondence course that Washington and Mallard had taken while enrolled at the junior college. Reid told her he knew they were taking that class, but really didn't have much knowledge about the class itself.

"I did what most good coaches do, I made sure my players were on track academically, but I was hired to coach basketball, which I did very well. I knew they were taking the correspondence class and I talked to them once or twice about it, but other than that I didn't have much involvement."

Matt chuckled inwardly. This was completely unexpected! Clearly Ken Reid didn't realize the amount of proof Matt had gathered.

Lisa continued with her questions.

"Tyron Washington told us that you helped them cheat in the classes. He said you arranged the whole thing. What would you say to that?"

Ken Reid smiled. "Are you saying that it is my word against a player who admitted he cheated? Doesn't that tell you all you should know? Tryon is a nice kid, but he never really understood that he had to make an effort to study. He barely got by no matter how much I helped him."

"I found Tyron to be very intelligent and highly credible," Lisa responded. "I have his story and wanted to get yours. Are you saying you categorically deny that you helped him with the correspondence course and that you have no knowledge of any cheating in that class?"

"That is exactly what I'm saying," Reid answered. "Anyone who says differently is a liar. It is my word against a player. I think a coach with my experience should carry more weight than a player who is telling you he cheated."

Lisa didn't answer right away so Matt spoke.

"Do you mind if I jump in here?" Matt asked.

"No, go right ahead," Lisa responded.

For the first time Ken Reid looked directly at Matt. There was a smirk on his face as he waited for Matt's question. Matt thought he would knock that smirk off right from the beginning.

"Coach Reid, you said you had no real involvement with the correspondence course, is that correct?"

"Yes, as I just said I knew they were taking the course, but I had no involvement with it."

Matt looked again at Reid. "Are you sure about that? You're sure you didn't have any more involvement than just knowing they were taking it?"

Reid looked annoyed. "I just told you that. Was I not clear? What are you having trouble understanding?"

Matt reached under his seat and pulled out his briefcase. Reid's face went pale as Matt began pulling out file folder after file folder.

"I think I should begin by saying I have copies of all of this material saved in very safe places." Matt looked directly at Reid as he said this. "So no matter what steps you may attempt to make, this will go directly to the NCAA and to GCSU."

"What do you have there?" Lisa asked.

Matt ignored her as he responded.

"Coach Reid," Matt looked him in the face as he spoke. "Here are copies of the assignments that Tyron Washington and Len Mallard completed to satisfy the requirements of the correspondence course. You will see they are done in the player's handwriting."

"Yes, because they did the work," Reid was worried, but continued to try to bluff.

"Yes, they did fill out the work," Matt said. "In their own words they would get copies of the assignments from you. There would be the original paper that they had to fill out as part of their work. One of the copies you gave to them would be the even numbered problems that had already been completed and the other copy would be the odd numbered problems that also had already been completed. They would then copy over the work onto their own papers. They said all of this was provided by you."

"That's a lie!" Reid shouted.

"Calm down Coach Reid," Matt kept going. "According to the players they would get these mysteriously filled out copies where one had the even numbered problems completed and the other had the odd numbered problems completed. It seemed strange to me."

"Yes, that makes no sense," Coach Reid stated.

"I have to agree Mr. Colter," Lisa Lasham echoed. "Why would they have odd and even numbered problems on different pages? This is just confusing the issue."

"I would have agreed with you had I stopped right there," Matt continued. "But I didn't stop right there. I found two young ladies named Trina Coker and Shelby Astle who helped me understand things better."

At the mention of the two names, Coach Reid began shaking. Matt saw that he was unnerved.

"Who are those women and what do they have to do with any of this?" Lisa asked.

"Let me continue, unless Coach Reid would like to tell us who they are?"

"I don't know anyone by those names," Reid said.

"That's funny, because they really knew you," Matt replied. "You see, Miss Lasham, those two young women were tutors at the junior college where Ken Reid worked and where Tyron Washington and Len Mallard played basketball. They were tutors for the basketball team. Both of the young ladies positively identified these papers," Matt paused while he pulled out the paperwork that the two young ladies had done.

"These papers are the odd-numbered problems that Coach Reid asked Trina Coker to complete and these are the even-numbered problems that Coach Reid asked Shelby Astle to complete. Both young ladies have told me the story and confirmed that this is their writing. Neither knew that Coach Reid would then have the players copy the answers in their own writing."

"You're trying to frame me," Coach Reid implored, but you could tell his heart wasn't in it any longer.

"Yes, I thought you might say something like that," Matt plowed on. "So I asked myself....self I said, even if all of this were true, the players would still need to take a final exam and wouldn't that exam have to be administered by someone with authority? Surely Ken Reid wouldn't be allowed to proctor a final exam."

Matt paused to look at Reid. It seemed that Reid knew what was coming and Matt knew he did because he had overheard the phone call from Josh Mayberry to Reid. Lisa had a stunned look on her face.

"So I did some work and found the actual final exam. I have the paperwork where you covered up the words FINAL EXAM and NAME and then made copies for the tutors. I have the work the young ladies did thinking they were helping show how to do the work on a homework assignment without knowing they were doing anything wrong. I was able to find the name of the person who proctored the exam. Josh Mayberry is very worried about what is going to happen to him."

Reid blanched at the mention of Mayberry's name.

"I wasn't sure what to do with Mayberry until I overheard a phone call he made asking for something to be done. You see, Mayberry confessed to his role in this whole circus. Since he made that call and since I was approached by some gentlemen who I believe meant me some harm, I'm going to make sure Mr. Mayberry's supervisors know of his role in this academic fraud."

"Wait a second," Lisa interrupted. "Who is Josh Mayberry? I'm afraid I'm a little behind here so help me get caught up."

"Would you like to explain Coach Reid or should I?" Matt asked.

Reid didn't respond so Matt continued.

"Josh Mayberry is the head of the math department at the junior college where Coach Reid coached. He was also the person who proctored the final exam in the correspondence course for Tyron Washington and Len Mallard. He has admitted that he didn't witness the final exam. You see, he was a little busy drinking beer and watching a game on the television with our friend Coach Reid here."

Lisa was stunned. Matt could tell she was both astonished at all of the new information and angry that she was only learning about it right now. Matt knew she would vent that anger on him when they were alone, but he gave her credit for keeping her composure while Coach Reid was present.

"So back to Coach Reid," Matt turned again to him. "Do you have anything you would like to add up to this point?"

"No, I have nothing to say. I want to terminate this interview until I have an attorney."

"That is fully within your rights Coach Reid," Lisa stated. "We'll terminate this interview right now."

With that she shut off her recorder. She wasn't sure what to do. Thankfully Ken Reid helped her out by getting up to leave. As he began walking towards the door, Shawn Morgan jumped up and told Reid that President Scott would like him to go to his office before leaving. Matt knew what was going to happen so he sat back down waiting for Lisa to erupt.

Shawn told them they could have the room as long as they needed, but excused himself and shut the door behind him as he left.

"What in the world do you think you are doing?" Lisa began the minute the door was closed. "You had all of this information and you didn't tell me a thing about it! I'm going to bring you up on charges."

Matt started laughing. He continued laughing as Lisa paused to look at him.

"What's so funny?" she asked.

"You are," Matt replied. "You are going to bring me up on charges? Charges of what? NCAA rules violations? I don't work for an NCAA school. If you try to take this out on GCSU, then we'll have a discussion with your supervisors and the NCAA Committee on Infractions about how this investigation unfolded. I will have to tell them that none of this would have been discovered if GCSU hadn't asked me to continue investigating, to find out more than the NCAA wanted."

Matt waited to let that sink in. "Now if we can continue, here are copies of everything I've discovered, the tests, the tutors completed odd and even assignments, copies of the interviews with the tutors and with Josh Mayberry. After you listen to the interviews and read the material I'll be happy to answer any questions you might have. You see, what you have here with GCSU, is a school that wants to do things right, but they don't just say that. They put their money and efforts where their mouth is. They instructed me to find the truth, no matter where it led me. I'm going to make sure the committee gives them credit for it."

Lisa took the materials and began packing up her backpack. She was fuming, but Matt knew she wasn't quite sure what to do. She thanked Matt for the paperwork and walked out without another word.

That hadn't gone well, but it hadn't gone as badly as he thought it might have. He sat there chuckling at the job he had. It might be tedious at times, but it was very interesting and he got to have fun once in a while. Today had been a fun day!

CHAPTER SEVENTEEN

Coach Reid had been asked to resign, which he did. He only had one month left on his contract and knew it wasn't in his best interest to try to fight so he packed up his things and left without saying a word. President Smith had convinced him that it would be in his best interests to leave quietly. Matt returned to his office, filled Ced and Holly in on what had happened over the past few days then tried to think of what to do.

"Surely, the NCAA will send a notice of allegations pretty soon," Holly said. "Do you want me to look around and see if I can find a rough draft on their computers?"

She laughed as she said it, but Matt knew she could probably hack her way in and find it if he asked her. Both knew that Matt would never ask her to do that, but she liked to push his buttons just for the fun of it.

They all brainstormed to see if there was anything else they needed to do. After talking it over they realized there was nothing for them to do. They were in the waiting period. The NCAA would send GCSU a notice of allegations and give the school a time period, usually 90 days, to respond to the charges in writing. Once the NCAA received the response, they would begin putting together the final documents for the Committee on Infractions.

The NCAA enforcement process was very different from a court case. The general public and media had little to no understanding how the NCAA process worked and the NCAA didn't really explain it. The NCAA staff would schedule a meeting with the school officials. In that meeting they would discuss the allegations one by one to try to discover where the NCAA and the school agreed and where unresolved issues remained. This was also the only real time a school could attempt to talk the enforcement staff out of a certain allegation. Matt had found these sessions to be very helpful with the more open minded NCAA directors of enforcement and a complete waste of time with other directors. It all depended upon the individual.

The final document was labeled the "Case Summary" and would include the NCAA enforcement staff's allegations, the responses from the school, a quick overview of whether or not the school and the enforcement staff agreed to the allegation and then any remaining issues. The enforcement staff would also be able to add relevant information that was reported or obtained by them.

Matt had always thought this document to be unfair to the schools. When he was at the enforcement staff he thought the NCAA received an unfair advantage by being able to summarize everything in one neat and tidy document. Sure, the school's written response was included and they could add anything, but the working document at the hearing was the case summary and that was written by the enforcement staff.

Now that Matt was on the side of the schools, he thought the document to be even more unfair. A school would have to give everything it had to the enforcement staff well before the hearing. It made things that much tougher on the school when it couldn't argue anything that the enforcement staff hadn't already seen and prepared for days or even weeks before the hearing.

Matt had learned a few tricks along the way. He would have to employ a few of them on GCSU's behalf.

The NCAA Committee on Infractions probably is the most misunderstood commitee at the NCAA. The general public has no real idea of how the hearings work or who is on the Committee. Most believe that the Committee is made up of NCAA employees, but that is completely untrue. The Committee on Infractions is made up of volunteers from schools around the nation as well as a few individuals completely outside the world of college athletics, such as judges or private attorneys.

The Committee members are appointed for three year terms with each term being renewable twice, so a Committee member could serve a total of nine years. The Committee usually meets six times a year. The meetings take place over weekends during which the Committee hears two to three cases. Serving on the Committee is a lot of work. Matt never understood why people wanted to serve on this Committee, but they never had a shortage of volunteers.

The Committee usually included a couple of Faculty Athletic Representatives or FARs as they are known in college athletics. Each school has a FAR, who is a professor working outside of athletics. The FAR's main charge is to look out for student-athlete welfare and they aren't beholden to the athletics department at the school.

Other members of the Committee would be made up of general counsel from a school, an athletics director or conference officials. There usually weren't any coaches on the Committee, but even more glaring to Matt was the fact that there were never any compliance people on the Committee. Matt thought that was appalling since the Committee had to dive into the world of compliance on almost every case. Would an attorney or FAR member know what was reasonable to expect from a school's compliance department? Take the recent phone call cases.

The compliance people would tell anyone who would listen that they could not possibly monitor every phone call made by every coach in every sport at their school. They also had to make sure everyone was educated, know which student-athletes had cars, where their families lived and worked, who they gave their tickets to and what relationship they may have, if any, to the student-athletes. The list of duties and things the compliance staff were supposed to be doing went on and on, but nobody ever thought about asking the compliance staff members what was realistic so the NCAA kept bringing charges of lack of institutional control or failure to monitor against schools and the Committee kept making findings of those allegations. The ironic thing is that neither the NCAA enforcement staff nor any member of the Committee had ever done any work on a campus compliance staff!

So Matt geared up for a battle. He knew that GCSU would be responsible for some of the things he was sure Lisa Lasham was going to allege, but this case was unique. Ken Reid had committed the most serious violations before he was employed at GCSU. As President Scott had said, GCSU was going to have to explain why they hired someone who would obviously be ripped apart during the hearing. Matt looked forward to the challenge.

Over the next couple of weeks Matt had many conversations with President Scott. As Matt already knew, Ken Reid was no longer a part of GCSU's basketball staff. Matt explained the waiting process, but President Scott was growing anxious. He wanted everything behind them.

At the end of the two-week period, Matt received yet another call from President Scott.

"Matt, I wanted to get your thoughts on the problems that might arise if I don't renew Randy Culp's contract. His contract is coming up at the end of this week and I have no intention of renewing him. What are our risks if we go ahead and let him know?"

Matt thought it over for a few seconds. "I guess the biggest risk is that Randy Culp gets angry and tries to harm GCSU by saying things to the NCAA that he knows will hurt. For instance, he might all of the sudden remember that there was an agreement with GCSU and Ken Reid that Reid would be hired if he brought players."

"What can we do to lessen the risks?" Scott asked.

"I'm not sure there is much we can do," Matt replied. "It couldn't hurt to call the NCAA to explain what you are going to do and explain that you are worried that Randy Culp might try to get revenge on GCSU."

"That's a good idea," Scott responded. "Can you set up a call with Miss Lasham at the NCAA? I'd like you to be on the call as well."

"May I make a suggestion?" Matt asked.

"Of course, that's why we work with you. What do you suggest?"

"I think we should ask for Miss Lasham's supervisor to be on the call. He is an old friend and is a little more experienced than Miss Lasham. He will understand our concerns and it will be good to go on the record with him."

"Sounds good, set it up and let me know when."

"Before you hang up President Scott, there is one more thing to consider," Matt informed him.

"Oh yeah? What is that?"

"Have you thought about how Ned McEnroe will take the news that you are terminating both of his assistant coaches? Like most head basketball and football coaches, he has an ego and may not like the fact that the university president is telling him he can't hire his own assistants."

"I'm counting on that," President Scott replied. "In fact, I'm hoping he has a big problem with it. The NCAA has this concept of institutional control and from what I've seen, most of big time college athletics fails right from the get go when you really look at it."

"In what way?" Matt asked.

"How much institutional control can there be when a basketball coach or football coach has more power, authority and earns more money than the president of the university? I would contend that any school that pays a coach more then his or her boss has, in essence, lost institutional control. I intend to let Coach McEnroe know that we have certain standards here that he must abide by. I've got to run, goodbye Matt"

Matt hung up the phone. He was growing to like Kevin Scott more and more. Sure, coaches were important and brought fame, prestige and notoriety to a university. Matt had listened to arguments from fans that coaches were more visible than a university president and more people knew who the coach was so they should make more money than the president, but Matt thought college athletics had gotten out of control decades ago. It was the price you pay to win in this day and age. Matt had no problems with coaches making great salaries, but with that salary comes greater responsibility to be on top of everything in the program and suffer the consequences when something went wrong.

A few more days went by then the NCAA Notice of Allegations finally arrived. It was sent to President Scott, but Matt received a copy as well. Matt looked through it to see what allegations the NCAA had made.

There was the initial allegation that GCSU had hired Ken Reid in a package deal that included him bringing two student-athletes with him. The allegation named Coach McEnroe and held him responsible, but it also named Randy Culp. That was interesting because it was basically saying that Randy Culp had some final authority on who was hired as the other assistant coach. Matt knew GCSU would deny that and point to the lack of any proof.

The significance that McEnroe and Culp were named in the allegations means that in NCAA terminology they could receive a "show cause" penalty. What that meant was that any institution that wanted to employ them would have to show cause to the Committee on Infractions why the school shouldn't receive a penalty for employing them. The Committee would penalize the school, not the coach. A "show cause" penalty really meant that the person under a show cause order would not be hired by an NCAA member school for the number of years attached to the show cause order.

Matt didn't think the NCAA had any proof so he wasn't too worried about that allegation though Coaches McEnroe and Culp would stress over it.

The second allegation was the academic fraud charge against Ken Reid. The school would have to respond to the charge and so would Ken Reid. The material the NCAA would use would be the material that Matt provided to them.

The third allegation was that GCSU had played two ineligible players, Tyron Washington and Len Mallard. GCSU would agree to that allegation, but would explain that it had no way of knowing the two players were ineligible because Ken Reid had covered the whole thing up. GCSU had lost in the first round of the tournament so there were no NCAA tournament games to forfeit. The NCAA might ask for monetary fine, but the money gained by playing in the tournament was divided amongst the members of GCSU's conference. If GCSU hadn't made the tournament, another team would have received the automatic entry so everyone would have received the same amount of money. Matt didn't think the Committee would ask for a monetary penalty because GCSU didn't receive any extra money because of the ineligible players.

The fourth allegation was an unethical conduct charge against Ken Reid. GCSU would agree completely with that allegation and let Ken Reid try to defend himself.

The final allegation was that GCSU lacked institutional control. That was a little surprising to Matt. He knew President Scott would be angry that the NCAA had alleged a lack of institutional control. Matt knew that was going to be a tough fight. If the NCAA said they lacked control because they hired a "rogue" coach who broke rules before coming in and didn't tell anyone while he was employed at GCSU, then Matt would have to show that GCSU had no way to prevent it and didn't lack control. Matt would need the compliance director, Shawn Morgan, to start compiling all educational material he had given as well as recreate any meetings he had conducted or spoke at involving compliance. Matt referred to that as the dog and pony show where a school was almost presumed guilty until it could prove its innocence.

Matt began drafting a response to the allegations. He worked closely with President Scott over the next two months until they agreed on the language and the appearance of the response. It was sent to the NCAA who spent a week going through it, then scheduled its pre-hearing conference with the school. Matt flew out once again to be on GCSU's campus when the NCAA arrived.

CHAPTER EIGHTEEN

Matt decided to check into a different hotel a little further away from campus for this visit. He wasn't worried about running into Ken Reid or Reid's friends who had attempted to attack him, but he thought it better to be safe than sorry. He met with President Scott to brief him on the pre-hearing conference routine the night before the meeting with the NCAA.

The following morning Ed Raines and Lisa Lasham were ushered into President Scott's office. Matt warmly greeted Ed and introduced him to Scott. He said hello to Lisa, but she only nodded, all business as usual. Ed began the meeting.

"First off President Scott I want to thank you for the heads up regarding the termination of Ken Reid and the nonrenewal of Randy Culp's contract. You were right, Culp did attempt to contact us. Miss Lasham explained that if he lied it would follow him to a future job and if he made up facts to get back at the school he could be charged with an unethical conduct charge. We never heard from him again, so I think we can agree that his first interview is what we will use in the hearing."

"I appreciate that Mr. Raines," President Scott said. "We don't think Randy did anything that violated NCAA rules, but I just decided that I wanted our basketball program to go in another direction. It was time for a change."

"We can understand that," Raines replied. "That leads us into the purpose of this pre-hearing conference. You have seen our notice of allegations, tell us what you thought of it and if there are areas you would like to discuss, now is the time."

Matt started to speak, but President Scott interrupted him.

"Before Mr. Colter starts, can I ask a sincere question?"

"Yes, of course, that is why we are here," Raines stated.

"I'm not intending to be rude and I hope this won't offend you," President Scott looked at both Raines and Lisa Lasham as he spoke. "Mr. Colter has told me that you are very fair and open-minded, but is there really any chance we can talk you out of any of these charges?"

"I don't take any offense and it is a fair question, but I'm not sure that the phrase 'talk you out of any of these charges' is the right phrase to use," Raines responded. "We are open to discussing any of the allegations and you can make your points and then we'll give you our thoughts. At the end of the day, if you can show us where an allegation maybe isn't merited we'll go back and reconsider it. We're only looking at what allegations we think we have evidence to prove to the Committee."

"Fair enough, go ahead Matt," President Scott directed.

"All right. Let's start with the first allegation. I don't think there is any evidence that anyone at GCSU orchestrated a package deal to hire Ken Reid as long as he brought the two young men with him. Unless I missed something in one of the interviews or you have additional information, I don't think there is anything that would lead one to conclude that there is proof to support that allegation."

Ed Raines listened to Matt then looked at Lisa Lasham. Matt could tell they had discussed it and he could tell that he had hit a nerve with Ed Raines. Matt thought that Lisa was going to reply, but Ed Raines spoke up.

"We hear what you are saying and to some extent we don't have much to add. I don't think you missed anything," Raines smiled at Matt. "In fact, knowing you, I'm sure you didn't miss anything. We concede this isn't the strongest allegation, but Lisa believes we need to at least present these allegations to the Committee to demonstrate how difficult they are to prove. I have discussed this with my superiors and to be perfectly honest there is a lot of disagreement about this. At the end of the day, the vice-president of enforcement supported bringing this allegation forward so it will be included, but just between us, I think this will be hard for the Committee to accept. We'll acknowledge in the hearing that there is no conclusive proof, but we'll make our best case."

President Scott spoke. "I appreciate your honesty and I hope you will appreciate mine. This seems a little ridiculous to me. I understand your position and that it is difficult to prove this type of allegation. You would need someone coming right out and admitting it, but my understanding doesn't permit me to say we will be happy to be the guinea pig on this."

"I can sympathize with your viewpoint," Raines said. "I will share your thoughts when I return to the NCAA headquarters, but I don't think they are going to persuade our vice-president to drop the allegation."

Matt asked for a minute to talk to President Scott. They left the room to speak in the hallway.

"This might not be a bad thing for us," Matt began. "If the NCAA is going to lead off with this allegation, we can use it to show that they are jumping to conclusions where they have no proof. This could backfire in a big way. I can also tell from Ed Raines' words that he doesn't agree with even bringing forward this allegation. He knows there is no proof, but obviously he lost that battle."

"Do you think this Lisa Lasham is the one who really wants it?"

"Yes, it has to be. Ed is smarter and knows the Committee will see there is no proof, but Lisa wants to establish a name for herself and is blinded by that. She thinks she can convince the Committee members, but her lack of experience is showing. The Committee won't make findings where there isn't proof. I think we should let this go."

"Okay Matt," President Scott replied. "This is why we retained you, but I hope you are right."

They re-entered the room. Matt could tell that Ed and Lisa had been discussing the allegation and Matt felt a little more tension between them.

"I think we understand your position," Matt stated. "We disagree with this on the very premise that the NCAA is bringing forward an allegation where there is no proof, but we appreciate your honesty. I want to be honest too. We are going to use everything at our disposal to refute this allegation. It might feel like we are getting a little personal, but it isn't personal from our side. Just as we can appreciate you taking this on as a bigger issue, we hope you can appreciate us using everything we can to fight for our athletics survival."

Matt let that sink in a bit. Lisa had no idea what he meant, but Matt could tell Ed Raines did. Matt never wanted to make things personal, but this case had a personal twist from the beginning because Lisa Lasham had failed to work in a cooperative manner.

"I think you are being a little melodramatic on this," Lisa Lasham replied. Matt ignored the comment, not taking the bait.

"One last point on this and then we can move on," Matt said. "You are charging both Ned McEnroe and Randy Culp in this allegation. I don't think I've ever seen a school where one assistant coach is responsible for the hiring of another assistant. Even though Randy Culp no longer is employed here, we owe it to him to try to have his name removed from this allegation."

Lisa spoke for the first time. "We included Randy Culp because he was the mastermind of the whole hiring. He and Ken Reid were good friends and we believe he arranged for Reid's hiring. His name will stay."

Matt saw the displeasure on Ed Raines' face as Lisa spoke. Matt didn't know what was going on, but somehow Ed Raines' had lost a little power on this case. Usually the person who worked the case would defer in these pre-hearing conferences to their director, who was their boss. Lisa and Ed obviously had some disagreement, but Lisa felt empowered to speak up against Ed's wishes. Matt thought it was a poor career choice for Lisa. Perhaps she had some sway with the vp of enforcement. Matt would have to figure that out.

"Is that the final NCAA word on that matter?" Matt asked looking at Ed.

"I'm afraid so," Raines stated as he looked down at the floor.

"Well then I think we have concluded our business," President Scott stated as he stood. "Thank you for coming all this way. We'll see you at the hearing."

He stretched out his hand towards Ed Raines who had a perplexed look on his face.

"But we've only gone through one allegation. We haven't discussed the other ones yet," Raines said.

"That's true, but from what I've seen on the discussion of the first allegation, I don't think we need to waste any more of any of our time. It appears that your mind is made up and we'll just bring it to the Committee. Thanks again for coming out."

Ed and Lisa stood up. They shook hands and quickly packed up their briefcases. Matt didn't say a word. He thought it was great that President Scott took charge like this. That would send a much more powerful message when Ed told the story back at NCAA headquarters.

As they left the room Matt walked with Lisa and Ed while President Scott remained behind. When they exited the building Ed gave Lisa the keys to the car.

"Lisa would you get the car? I'd like to have a word with Matt before we leave."

Lisa didn't like that, but there was little she could do. Ed was her boss so she took the keys and walked towards the parking lot.

"Matt, I want to apologize to you," Ed began. "I trust you enough that I'm going to tell you something and ask you not to repeat it at the hearing. If you do, I'll have to deny it. You guys are absolutely right. There is no proof to allegation number one. I told our vp that, but Lisa made her argument to include it and somehow she persuaded the vp to include it."

"She can be persuasive," Matt chuckled. "She is young and wants to make a name for herself, but she is in too much of a hurry. I've tried to befriend her, but she wants nothing to do with me."

Ed laughed. "You are right, she wants nothing to do with you. She thinks you are evil."

"She is going to think I'm the devil at the hearing. I have to let you know that I'm going to be much more aggressive defending GCSU than you are used to seeing from me. This is a school and Kevin Scott is a president trying to do things the right way. They don't deserve getting hammered. Lisa has been a little sloppy and I'm going to have to point that out to the Committee."

Ed looked at Matt. "I understand, you have to do what you have to do. Can you tell me something? Have I been negligent in my supervision of this case? I'm only asking because I want to know if I'm slipping."

Matt thought about it for a moment. "Ed, I can't answer that for sure. I think it is probably a situation where you are not being told some things so you are going to most likely be surprised at the hearing by some of what I say, but I think it will reflect poorly on Lisa. I wanted you to know that in advance because I respect you and enjoy working with you."

"Thanks for that, but I must say I'm a little worried," Raines stated. "You have always been very fair and have gone out of your way to not attack the NCAA or the enforcement staff. The fact that you are warning me makes me think some trouble is coming our way."

"I don't know if it is that dramatic, but I do think Lisa has been rushing to make a name for herself and didn't do some things she should have. I hope once this is all over with I can sit down with you and share some observations."

"Matt, I'd like that. Good luck in your defense and thanks for letting me know."

They shook hands and Matt watched Raines walk to the car. He felt a little sorry for him because Ed Raines was a true believer in the NCAA mission. He wasn't good at playing backroom politics, but it appeared that Lisa Lasham was quite adept in that skill.

Matt went back to speak with President Scott.

"Matt I apologize if I ruined anything you had planned, but it was plain to me that we were wasting our time trying to get them to move off of anything."

Matt smiled. "Don't worry one bit, I think this was very helpful."

President Scott seemed perplexed as he asked, "Helpful? In what way was this helpful? I think I probably offended them and we accomplished nothing."

"That is where you are wrong," Matt stated. "We accomplished quite a bit. I just had a little discussion with Ed Raines. I can tell there is a big disagreement at the NCAA about all of this. There is no proof about allegation one and Ed knows it. He has been overruled, which helps me see that the NCAA enforcement staff isn't being as careful as they normally are. That will play to our advantage. We can set the tone with allegation number one that will carry through the entire hearing."

Matt waited to see if President Scott wanted to opine on what Matt had just said. After a few seconds of silence Matt continued.

"The other thing that we accomplished here is that I am completely free to take the gloves off when it comes to Lisa Lasham's handling of the case. I usually give some professional courtesy to the enforcement staff because they have a very difficult job and I like a lot of them. Lisa Lasham's aggressive pursuit of this case and her failure to follow up on getting additional information combined with your leadership to get that same information even if it hurts GCSU will play to our advantage. I was struggling trying to figure out how to present that to the Committee without burning too many bridges with the enforcement staff, but now, because of what I have seen today, I can go ahead and be as aggressive as I want."

"Well that is good, I guess," President Scott responded. "You are the expert when it comes to these hearings, but I want to take an active part."

"That is exactly what I need you to do. The president of the university always is asked to attend the hearing. Normally they make an opening statement regarding the university and its commitment to the rules then they hand it off and sit silently through the rest of the hearing. I think it will impress the Committee if we have you speaking throughout the defense."

Matt was excited. This hearing was going to be a little different than normal and he finally had a president who was fully engaged!

CHAPTER NINETEEN

Matt spent the next few weeks working with President Scott and the AD Mike Love, preparing them for the upcoming NCAA Committee on Infractions hearing. The more time Matt spent around Mike Love, the less he liked him. Love was one of those type of people who said whatever he thought his supervisor wanted to hear. In this case, his supervisor was the president of the university.

It seemed to Matt that President Scott was much more in tune to things like that and Matt was surprised that Mike Love hadn't been exposed before this. That wasn't really Matt's concern so he focused on getting them ready for the hearing.

The Committee on Infractions had requested that President Scott, Mike Love and the compliance director Shawn Morgan attend the hearing along with Coach McEnroe. They, along with Matt would make up GCSU's contingent. Randy Culp had been asked to appear. GCSU had informed Culp that it would pay for him to attend the hearing.

GCSU was under no obligation to pay for Culp's expenses. He had concluded his contract and was no longer employed at GCSU. Many other schools would not have paid for the travel expenses of a staff member no longer employed, especially if they thought that staff member may try to hurt them during the hearing. Matt had raised that point with President Scott, but he had informed Matt that he was going to continue doing what he thought was the ethical thing, even if it did hurt.

The Committee had also requested that Ken Reid attend the hearing, but Matt knew that Reid had not responded to anything regarding the upcoming hearing. The NCAA had sent a notice of allegations to all of the coaches. McEnroe and Culp had received the allegations that concerned them. Reid had received the allegations involving the academic fraud and playing the ineligible players as well as his unethical conduct allegation.

McEnroe and Culp had each sent in a written response to the allegations, but Reid had not responded at all. Reid also gave no indication that he would attend the hearing. Matt was happy with that because GCSU was going to lay most of the blame directly at Reid's feet. Having him not in attendance would prevent the arguments that might have resulted between them in front of the Committee.

The week before the hearing, Matt again was on GCSU's campus to meet with President Scott and Mike Love. This time Ned McEnroe was going to be included. Matt understood that McEnroe had retained his own attorney and Matt thought it would be a good idea to sit down with everyone to go over things to see if they were on the same page.

They all gathered in a conference room outside of President Scott's office. Matt introduced himself to Ned McEnroe again and to McEnroe's attorney.

"Let me start off by explaining how the room will be laid out," Matt began. "The hearing is very different from a court of law. There is no witness stand and no gallery. The room is set up in a big hollow square. The Committee members will be on one side of the square. To their left at the next side will be the NCAA staff. The vice-president for enforcement will be the first person. Next to her will be Lisa Lasham, the investigator assigned to the case. Next to Lisa will be Ed Raines, Lisa's supervisor and the supervisor on the case. The rest of the side will be made up of various NCAA enforcement staff directors and a few new staff members. They are there to observe and most likely won't say a thing.

"To the Committee's right will be us. President Scott will be first. I'll sit next to him, then Mike Love will be on my right. Shawn Morgan will be on Love's right. Then it will be Coach McEnroe and your attorney sitting next to Shawn. Randy Culp and his attorney will be on the other side of you.

"The fourth side of the square, facing opposite of the Committee is for people involved who are no longer affiliated with the university. Randy Culp may choose to sit there with his attorney. It appears that Ken Reid won't be attending, but if he does show up he will be sitting there. A couple of NCAA staff members who are responsible for the room and the set-up will be on that side as well. In the middle of the square will be a stenographer, or what you see in the movies as a court reporter. He will be recording the entire proceeding."

"So why would you have Randy Culp sit with GCSU's side?" McEnroe interrupted. "If he is no longer with the university then why would he be at our table?"

"Do you object to having him there?" Matt asked.

"No, not in the least," McEnroe responded. "In fact, I wish he was still my assistant coach." He looked at Mike Love who wouldn't meet his gaze. Love looked at the floor.

"In fact, it is pretty hypocritical to have Randy sit with us like we are one happy family," McEnroe continued. "We shouldn't try to be painting a happy face on the situation. Let the Committee know how it is."

President Scott looked squarely at Ned McEnroe.

"Coach McEnroe," Scott started. "It was my decision to not renew Randy Culp's contract. As the president of the university I have final say on hiring. I decided that Randy Culp was not the right person to be our assistant coach. You may not agree with that, but that is not up for debate. I hope you understand, GCSU is going to argue in support of Randy Culp. We are going to say he is innocent of the allegation against him. That is why he will have the option to sit with us or sit at the other side of the square."

Scott stared at McEnroe as he spoke. Matt thought that this was the President Scott he needed in the hearing. He was a man of conviction and didn't shy away from a fight. Matt decided it was time to sit quietly. Mike Love still had not looked up from the floor. McEnroe wasn't backing down.

"I've never heard of a school where the university president tells the head basketball coach who he can and can't hire as assistant coaches."

"Well you are hearing of it now," Scott replied. "I won't stand for having people represent this university who are not the type of people I want working for us, especially in something as visible as our basketball program. It was the people you brought in who got us into this mess."

"I didn't know Ken Reid very well," McEnroe chirped.

"Exactly!" President Scott stared straight at McEnroe.

"You can't hold me responsible for someone doing something without my knowledge. I had no idea what Coach Reid had done!"

"Coach McEnroe, we can talk all day about who should be ultimately responsible for the mess we are in. I hold you, in part, responsible because you brought those people here just as Mike Love is responsible for bringing you here and I am responsible for bringing Mike Love here. I take that responsibility, I own it, but I'm not going to make that mistake again. Any new assistants you hire will be approved by me. They will have advanced degrees and will be teachers first and foremost."

McEnroe looked aghast. "How do you expect me to win under those restrictions?"

"We don't let our university departments hire people without advanced degrees so why should we let our athletics department? You are paid more than our professors who have doctorate degrees and your assistants are as well. I understand that athletics is a different world, but if we want that world to co-exist in our academic setting, then I want to be comfortable with who we have working there. I may relax the rules after you have proven yourself, but for now that is the standard!"

Everyone sat in silence for about thirty seconds. Then Ned McEnroe stood up. "I don't think I want to work any longer at this university. I quit!"

President Scott didn't miss a beat. He pulled out a folder then took a prepared piece of paper out of that folder.

"Here is a typed resignation letter," he stated. "Read through it and if you agree with it sign it where indicated."

"Ned, as your attorney I have to caution you," McEnroe's attorney started.

Before he could continue McEnroe interrupted.

"Be my attorney by sitting there and shutting up," he said. McEnroe grabbed a pen, signed the resignation letter and threw the pen down on the table.

"As for this hearing, don't expect me to show up. I'm done with GCSU and I'm done coaching!"

McEnroe stormed from the room. His attorney looked sheepishly at the group. "I guess he just forfeited his last year of salary. I need to rethink who I represent."

The attorney let the room.

The atmosphere in the room was electric. Matt could feel the energy, but Mike Love only worried about himself. He looked at President Scott trying to figure out what to say.

President Scott gathered up the signed resignation letter. He sank back down into his chair reading through the letter.

"Hmm, that went rather well," he stated. "Thank you Mr. Colter for preparing this letter for me. Mike, we'll have to discuss what we are looking for in a new coach. I have some very specific qualities in mind."

Love, always the pleaser responded. "Yes sir, I keep a list of candidates that can build upon the success we've had. We went to the NCAA tournament for the first time so we should be able to pick from a more qualified list of candidates."

"That may be true," President Scott replied. "But you and I will have to first have an understanding of what I expect from coaches who represent this great university. Our students and faculty demand that and I won't tolerate less."

"Yes sir," Love eeked out. "I will find the right person."

Matt went through what would take place at the hearing one more time. They had rehearsed who would speak at what time. Each allegation would be discussed. Matt had prepared Shawn Morgan for questions he might receive. President Scott had instructed Mike Love to only answer when asked a direct question. Matt thought that the less Mike Love spoke the better. He told Love there would be a pad of paper in front of him and that he should write anything he thought he should say down first so Matt could read it.

"Remember one thing," Matt told Love. "When you speak in that hearing, you are drawing attention to yourself. That will only invite more questions. You may think you can charm your way through the hearing, but I am telling you directly that you can't. They see through everything. Your best strategy would be to never talk unless asked a direct question to you. If you went through the entire hearing without having to say a word, that would be a successful hearing for you."

Love nodded. Matt could tell he had put some fear in Love. Matt thought they were as ready as they could be.

The following week the group flew to Indianapolis, home of the NCAA. The hearings rotated locations, but half of them were in Indianapolis and GCSU had drawn that location. Matt enjoyed going to Indianapolis. The downtown had a nice feel to it and the people were friendly. There were also lots of great restaurants.

President Scott, Love, Shawn Morgan and Matt went to dinner at the famous St Elmo's steakhouse the night before the hearing. They enjoyed a great steak dinner and were exiting the restaurant when they ran into Randy Culp.

"So dinner before the execution," Culp joked.

"Hello Randy," Mike Love replied. Love looked very nervous. Matt knew that Love and Culp had been friendly. Matt could only imagine the stress Love felt hoping that Culp wouldn't do or say anything to cause problems. Would he do something that hurt Love's position with the university? Culp was the real wild card in this whole hearing.

"Hello Mike," Culp said. "I see the group is all here except for the coaches. You know, I may have to clarify a few things from my interview during the hearing tomorrow."

Love visibly reacted by drawing back. Matt stepped forward.

"Hi, Mr. Culp. Matt Colter," Matt extended his hand.

"Yes I remember you from the interview," Culp looked at Matt skeptically not returning the handshake.

"I just wanted to remind you of something," Matt stated. "You are on the record giving your version of events. If you change your story, it could hurt GCSU."

Before Matt could continue Culp jumped in.

"Yes Sherlock, I know that. Why do you think I'm enjoying myself so much. If I hurt GCSU, what is that to me? You guys let me go, I don't owe you anything."

"I'm not talking about anyone owing anyone else. I just want to make sure you understand something," Matt paused to make sure Culp was listening. "If you change your story, GCSU could be hurt a little bit. Depending upon what you say, the Committee may take away an official visit or two from prospects or reduce the number of recruiting days the staff will have on the road. But think about what might happen to you. You will be indicting yourself. You would most likely get a 'show cause' order against you, meaning you will not be allowed to coach at an NCAA school for a number of years. You would also be cited for unethical conduct for not being truthful in the first interview. That would extend your penalty. Now we want you to be honest and tell the truth, but we also want you to understand the consequences if you make things up just to hurt GCSU."

Matt began walking away. His group followed him leaving Randy Culp standing on the sidewalk staring furiously at them.

"That was perfect Matt," President Scott said as they walked. "That will give Mr. Culp plenty to think about."

They returned to the hotel, ready to see what tomorrow would bring.

CHAPTER TWENTY

NCAA Committee on Infraction hearings are not open to the public. There is little to no explanation about what happens during a hearing so it is one of the most misunderstood processes in existence. The NCAA, in an effort to be more open, recently tried to show to a group of media how the NCAA hearing process worked. There were a flurry of articles written, but it was clear from the articles that there was still no real understanding of the Committee on Infractions hearing process.

The NCAA has breakfast available for all who will be in attendance, which is the NCAA staff members, the Committee on Infraction members and the school under fire. That makes for an interesting setting. Each person tries to be cordial and polite, but the people from the school are always nervous and not sure exactly what to do. Some of the NCAA enforcement staff, who have worked with that particular school and at least know them, try to engage in small talk, but it is just an awkward setting. It would be like having a judge sit down to breakfast with the prosecuting attorneys, the defense attorneys and the defendant.

Often the school elects to not participate in the breakfast, entering the room just a few minutes before the scheduled start time. President Scott had elected to have his group show up at 7:00 am to eat the breakfast and talk to whomever they could. He reasoned that it wouldn't hurt to have the Committee members at least have a brief introduction to them before the hearing began.

Matt was familiar with all of the senior enforcement staff so he walked around saying hello. He also knew several members of the Committee since he appeared before them frequently with schools. He noticed that Lisa Lasham sat at her assigned seat going over her notes. She seemed a bit nervous, but Matt thought she should at least come over to say hello to President Scott and Mike Love. Ed Raines said hello to everyone and showed them where they could get the food.

Matt thought it was a good idea to have his group come into the room early to see how it was laid out and get comfortable. Matt had explained to them that there would be a microphone at each seat. When you spoke you had to remember to push the button on your microphone, which would then cut off everyone else's microphone. It was tricky because people kept cutting each other off inadvertently, but eventually everyone got the hang of it.

They all ate breakfast and chatted amicably. The Committee members were comfortable because they attended these hearings six times a year. The NCAA enforcement staff was comfortable because they also attended six times a year, at least the senior enforcement staff members. The most nervous people in the room were the group from GCSU who might only attend one hearing in their lifetime and Lisa Lasham. Lisa had presented in front of the Committee before, but it was always nerve wracking to present your case and know people would try to tear it down.

In this case, Lisa was even more nervous because she knew that Matt would try to demonstrate her mistakes. Ed Raines had told her that Matt was very good and that Matt wouldn't go after an enforcement staff member unless he felt it was warranted. Given that Matt had specifically told Ed that he would be talking about how Lisa handled the case and Ed had told Lisa about it, Lisa was even more nervous.

Matt wandered over to Lisa's seat and stood in front of her. She was pouring over her notes and failed to notice Matt. He finally cleared his throat, which made her look up.

"Hello Miss Lasham," Matt stated. "Nice to see you. Good luck today and I want to apologize in advance for anything I say that might offend you."

Matt wasn't trying to unnerve her. He honestly felt sorry for what he thought might happen. He was stepping out of his normal routine because he felt he had no other choice. He owed it to GCSU to provide them the best defense he could and in this case, that meant that he might have to paint Lisa in a negative light.

"Good luck to you as well," Lisa replied trying to display a confidence she didn't feel. "I also want to say there is nothing personal. The people from GCSU seem like nice enough people, but I have my job to do."

"Yes, I understand that, as do I," Matt stated. "Perhaps when this is all over we can sit down to discuss things. I would be happy to offer opinions or share thoughts from the other side of things to help you get a better understanding of their side."

"Thanks, but I don't think I'll need that. Why would I want to get a better understanding of the other side? I don't want to let sympathy dissuade me from doing my job."

"I've always thought that understanding the complete picture made you a better investigator," Matt stated. "Remember when I said that the job of the enforcement staff was to gather evidence even if it helped exonerate a school? I truly believe that and think that you should remember that from time to time."

Lisa was trying to control her temper. This man was so smug, he thought he knew so much. Lisa would enjoy taking him down a peg.

"Well, good luck again, now I need to go back to reviewing my notes."

With that Lisa sat back down dismissing Matt. He shrugged and walked back to his group. Ed Raines noticed the exchange wondering what had been said. He knew Matt Colter, considered him a friend. Ed was worried that Lisa had made this too personal, but he didn't understand why.

The Committee Chair asked for everyone to take their seats. Each seat had a name card in front so that everyone could see the name of every other person in the room. The Chair spent the first ten minutes explaining the procedures. Matt had heard this routine a number of times so he spent the time looking around the room.

President Scott was ready. Mike Love was already sweating and it was only 8:00 am, Shawn Morgan was nervous, but that was understandable. There would be a certain amount of nerves for everyone.

Coach McEnroe and Ken Reid had chosen to not attend so there were a lot of empty spots at the tables. Randy Culp had not come with an attorney, which didn't surprise Matt. Randy seemed like the type who was both cheap and thought he could do things better than anyone else. Randy had also chosen to sit, not with the GCSU group, but at the table facing the Committee. He was alone on one end of the table with a few NCAA staff members sitting at the other end of his table.

The NCAA enforcement staff members sat comfortably. The only ones who would speak would be Lisa Lasham and Ed Raines. The VP of enforcement would introduce the members of enforcement who were in attendance. The VP would then turn it over to Ed, who would give an overview of the case. Ed would then turn it over to Lisa, who would do the majority of the talking. The other directors of enforcement were observers. They wouldn't speak unless asked a direct question by a Committee member.

The Chair of the Committee was concluding the opening by explaining how the microphones worked. Matt had briefed his group ahead of time because this was always an issue. If you had a group conversation you could observe that people wanted to jump in to say things. With a microphone in front of each person the temptation to push your button to talk was great, but when you pushed your button it cut off everyone else's microphone, including the person who was speaking at the moment. People cut each other off accidentally until they got used to the system.

The Chair turned to the vp of enforcement and asked for the NCAA opening. The VP introduced the group they had in the room, which were all of the directors of enforcement, the new employees who were observing this as part of their training, the staff members who were assisting the investigators and then Ed and Lisa. Ed then gave a quick overview of the case.

Matt thought it was interesting that when Ed started talking about the hiring process he said it was often difficult if not impossible to prove that a school had an arrangement with someone if it wasn't in writing. He acknowledged that the NCAA had no proof regarding this allegation, but that the enforcement staff thought it was important to engage the Committee in a discussion regarding the subject. Ed gave a brief outline of the other allegations then stopped talking and sat down.

The Chair turned to GCSU's table and asked for an opening statement. Matt had explained to President Scott that this was usually the time for the university president to talk about his or her school and declare their commitment to compliance with NCAA rules. President Scott had decided upon a different approach and worked it out with Matt in advance.

"Committee members and NCAA staff," President Scott began. "I know this is usually the time to talk all about my school. I am proud to be the president of such a fine university. But rather than waste everyone's time talking about our school I would rather use this time to talk about the case."

The Committee members set up a little straighter in their seats. They were used to hearing a president drone on about the size of the student population or hear about esteemed alumni from the school. This was a new approach and they were interested.

"I can appreciate the tough job the NCAA enforcement staff has," President Scott continued. "Our attorney here, Matt Colter, used to work for the staff and he has nothing but the utmost respect and admiration for the job they do. He has told me about their work until I have started to understand and appreciate their position. But that admiration doesn't extend to allowing our school to be maligned for something we think didn't happen. The discussion surrounding allegation one is a discussion that perhaps the Committee and the staff should have, but not with our reputation at stake. You heard Mr. Raines say there is no proof and we agree. We think that allegation should be dropped right at the outset."

This was definitely a different approach and the Committee members looked at each other not sure who should speak. Before anyone said anything President Scott continued on.

"Now that is something we can all talk about as we get into the actual details of the allegation. I understand that and apologize for jumping the gun. The other allegations are for the most part the actions of an individual who we agree, committed academic fraud before he arrived at GCSU without anyone's knowledge at GCSU. I contend that we are guilty of hiring an individual who didn't turn out to be the type of person our coaches thought he was. Please keep in mind that the NCAA didn't uncover this academic fraud. I believe they will acknowledge that this would not have been uncovered if we hadn't asked our attorney to pursue anything and everything. He is the person who found out about the academic fraud, he is the person who found the people to interview.

"I understand that the Committee considers the school's cooperation when discussing the penalties and corrective actions. I would ask you to keep in mind that we not only cooperated, we didn't just sit still when the NCAA had come to an end. We continued forward and uncovered much of what will be discussed today. Rather than get a pat on the back as credit, I ask the Committee to really think about sending a message to schools that they can help themselves by going above and beyond what is expected. Send a message that educational institutions won't just get an atta boy, but will get real consideration for working with the enforcement staff to uncover violations."

President Scott let that sink in before continuing. Matt could see that the Committee members were not put off by Scott's comments. Hopefully they would consider it even more coming from a university president.

Scott continued. "Let me introduce everyone in our group, next to me is our attorney Matt Colter, whom I assume most of you know. Next to Matt is our director of athletics Mike Love and our director of compliance Shawn Morgan. I want to thank the enforcement staff for their hard work and for being patient with us. And I want to thank the Committee for considering our case today."

President Scott stopped talking and looked at the Committee. He could see he had their attention so he smiled and sat down.

Matt looked around the room. The enforcement directors didn't look happy, but they were looking at Lisa and not at the GCSU group. The Committee members were sitting back contemplating what President Scott had said.

The Chair finally pushed his microphone button. "Mr. Culp, would you like to introduce yourself and make an opening statement?"

Randy Culp still had that same smirk on his face. Matt watched him closely, unsure of what he would say.

"Hello everyone," Culp began. "My name is Randy Culp and I am a former assistant basketball coach at GCSU. I am happy to hear that my former school is agreeing that I didn't enter into any type of agreement with Ken Reid to hire him in exchange for him bringing players. As I mentioned during the interview, I knew that Reid had his players, but there was no agreement. I'll save my other remarks for later."

The opening was finished. Now the Committee Chair would have Lisa introduce the first allegation. He turned to the NCAA table.

"Before we begin allegation number one, I'd like to ask the staff to address the comments made by President Scott, namely do you have any evidence whatsoever that there was an agreement in place for GCSU to hire Ken Reid as an assistant basketball coach in exchange for Reid bringing the two players..." the Chair referred to his notes. "Yes here it is, the two players Tyron Washington and Len Mallard to GCSU."

Ed looked at Lisa and Lisa looked at Ed. Matt knew that something very important was happening and the Committee members were picking up on the fact that the NCAA enforcement staff was unsure of what to say. This would only help GCSU's entire case. Finally Ed pushed the button on his microphone and spoke.

"Mr. Chair, the NCAA doesn't have a smoking gun, this isn't a case of anyone admitting this. Ken Reid was hired by GCSU and Ken Reid did bring two very good players with him, but no, we have no proof."

"Then please help the Committee understand why we should not just toss this allegation out right now?"

Lisa pushed her microphone button. "If I could address this to the Committee?"

The Chair looked at her and said, "Yes, please go ahead."

"I pushed to include this allegation because I think it is reasonable to conclude that this occurred. The coaches all acknowledged that they knew there were two good players at the junior college where Ken Reid coached. It is reasonable to assume that they considered that when they looked at whom to hire as an assistant coach."

Matt was going to jump in to the discussion, but the Committee Chair beat him to the punch.

"To make sure I understand this completely, you are saying that there is no real proof other than an assumption that the coaching staff knew about the two good players? Is that correct?"

"Yes Mr. Chair," Lisa replied. "You can see how difficult it is to prove an allegation of this type. Unless someone comes right out and admits it, then we will never be able to prove these allegations."

The Chair addressed Ed Raines. "Mr. Raines, you agreed to include this allegation?"

Matt knew that put Ed in a very tough spot. Ed hadn't agreed to it, he had been overruled. Matt thought that the vp of enforcement might say something, but Ed was left on his own.

"We discussed it at length," Ed responded. "At the end of the day, the allegation was included so I have to take responsibility for that and say I agreed to include it."

The Chair was experienced enough to know that something was fishy here, but he didn't think now was the time to address it. He had seen enough of Ed Raines to know that Ed wouldn't point fingers at anyone else, but the Chair also could tell that Raines' heart wasn't in this fight.

"Based on what we've heard, I'd like to see if any member of the Committee would object to throwing out allegation number one right here." The Chair paused to look at the other Committee members who shook their heads.

"Okay, allegation one is no longer a part of this case. Let's move on to allegation number two."

Matt spoke up before Lisa could begin allegation number two.

"If I can interject something here," Matt began. "Since allegation number one is the only allegation that mentions Mr. Culp, we'd like to ask for him to be excused at this point."

Randy Culp jumped out of his seat. He didn't bother to push the microphone button. "I want to stay for the whole hearing. I worked at the school and I want to hear what is said."

"Mr. Culp," the Chair calmly said. "Mr. Colter is correct. You are no longer at risk, you have won and will suffer no penalties. It is a good time to leave while you are ahead."

The room laughed, but Randy Culp wasn't laughing.

"You mean to tell me that I flew all the way to Indianapolis for a hearing and I'm dismissed within the first half hour? What about my time? I want to stay for the rest of the hearing."

"Perhaps the NCAA will be held responsible for picking up your travel costs," the Chair stated. "That might teach them to carefully consider the consequences of including an allegation that they acknowledge has no proof."

"GCSU paid for my travel and I don't care about that. I want to stay!" Culp shouted.

"I'm sorry Mr. Culp, that is not how these hearings work. You are allowed to stay for any part where you are personally named in the allegation, but since we've dropped allegation one you are free and clear. I have to ask you to leave."

Randy Culp stared furiously at the Committee. Matt wasn't sure what he would do, but Culp realized he had no choice. Culp gathered his belongings and left the room knocking over his chair as he exited.

"We usually don't take a break this early into the hearing, but I think we should take a ten minute break right now," the Chair said. "I'd like to talk with the senior enforcement staff members over in that corner.

Matt could tell that things had started very badly for the enforcement staff, but couldn't have been better for GCSU. The first allegation had been dropped, the Committee was upset with the enforcement staff for including it. Randy Culp had been dismissed and would no longer be a risk during the hearing. President Scott had already given notice that he was a president who would be very involved in the discussions. Yes, Matt thought. This couldn't have started any better. I just hope it continues going our way!

CHAPTER TWENTY ONE

During the break, the Chair of the Committee and the other Committee members met with the vp of enforcement and the directors of the enforcement staff. Matt could see that the Chair was doing all of the talking. Lisa Lasham wasn't included in the discussion so she sat at her chair looking down at her notes. She had to know that what was being said in the corner reflected poorly on her decision to push to include the first allegation.

Finally the side meeting broke up and the senior enforcement officials having been thoroughly chastised, returned to their seats. The Chair and the other Committee members also returned to their seats. Matt smiled at President Scott, but they didn't speak during the break. They had their plan and were going to stick to it. So far it had worked to perfection!

The Chair called the meeting back to order and asked Lisa Lasham to present the second allegation.

"Yes sir," Lisa started nervously. "Allegation two is an academic fraud charge against former assistant coach Ken Reid. You see how it is outlined before you on paper. The institution is in agreement to the facts of this allegation. Ken Reid has chosen to not participate in these proceedings nor did he provide a written response. The enforcement staff is ready to answer any questions."

There was a moment of silence to see if any of the Committee members had any questions. The Chair turned to GCSU's group. "Does anyone from GCSU have any comments to make?"

President Scott pushed the button on his microphone. Matt had planned to have President Scott take the lead on this allegation for strategic reasons Matt hoped would play in GCSU's favor.

"Thank you Mr. Chair," President Scott said. "GCSU is in agreement to the facts of this allegation. However, we are unclear if this is a violation of NCAA rules since Ken Reid committed this academic fraud while working at a junior college. There was no involvement from anyone at GCSU. We aren't downplaying the seriousness of what happened here. It is a travesty for many reasons that we can discuss and have outlined in our written response. But at the end of the day we aren't sure if it is an NCAA violation because it didn't happen under NCAA jurisdiction."

The Chair turned to the enforcement staff. "Does the staff have any response to this? Do you believe this is an NCAA violation and if so, why? President Scott makes a good point that this didn't happen at an NCAA school with NCAA student-athletes or coaches. Does the staff have any way to tie this to GCSU?"

Lisa jumped to speak. "This allegation was included because we believed that GCSU knew exactly what Ken Reid was doing. They were in discussions to hire him around this time frame. We have nothing that can prove that anyone at GCSU directed Ken Reid to do this, but we do believe someone had knowledge or should have known what was happening."

The Committee member who was a private attorney asked a simple direct question. "What proof do you have that anyone from GCSU was involved in this other than a suspicion? This is a very serious allegation and I need more than a suspicion to link this to a university."

Lisa looked through her notes. She conferred with Ed Raines who really had nothing to help her. Looking frustrated she finally answered.

"We concede that we hadn't thought about this happening outside of NCAA jurisdiction. The academic fraud was committed, GCSU agrees to that. It was committed by a coach GCSU soon employed and involved student-athletes that soon represented the university in competition. We believe that is enough to tie it to GCSU."

Another Committee member, one of the FARs who was a law professor at his school, responded. "Miss Lasham, you are making some big leaps to get to the point where you lay blame at the doorstep of GCSU. I think it is a tough hurdle you are attempting to jump to put responsibility on their shoulders, but before you even get to that discussion, you haven't really rebutted the claim that this occurred outside of NCAA jurisdiction. Now we will get to the third allegation, that GCSU competed ineligible players, in a minute and that might be a more appropriate starting point because I don't see any basis to conclude that allegation two is an NCAA violation."

He sat back in his chair. The Committee looked at the NCAA enforcement staff group waiting for a response. Lisa had no idea what to say. Finally Ed Raines jumped to the rescue.

"We present this allegation to the Committee to consider. If you conclude that this occurred outside of the NCAA jurisdiction, we wouldn't have a problem with that, but we thought it was important to discuss it now so there would be an understanding for the third allegation."

"Mr. Raines," the Chair replied. "I can appreciate your attempt to salvage what has been a disastrous start, but you would have to agree that you could have introduced this fraud without making it a formal allegation, right?"

Ed smiled and nodded at the Chair. Matt was very happy and would have just stopped right there, but President Scott wanted to make another point.

"Mr. Chair, if I could add one more thing?"

"President Scott, go right ahead," the Chair responded. "So far you have been the only one making pertinent points today." The Committee smiled in unison.

"When I opened the discussion today," Scott started. "I mentioned that I would like the Committee to really think about what it meant to give credit to a school that not only cooperates, but drives much of the investigation."

President Scott paused to make sure he had the full attention of the Committee. Matt took that moment to look at the Committee members. Most were sitting forward in their seats. Many were taking notes, but all were listening very attentively.

"It is my understanding and the NCAA can correct me if I'm wrong," Scott continued. "It is my understanding that the NCAA made an attempt to speak to the two former student-athletes in this case, Tyron Washington and Len Mallard. The NCAA was unsuccessful in reaching them and told our attorney Mr. Colter, that it had exhausted all available avenues to contact those former student-athletes. GCSU could have stopped right there and all we would have before us today is allegation number one that was thrown out and perhaps an institutional control allegation that would have been difficult to prove when there were no allegations of NCAA violations.

"GCSU is committed to abiding by NCAA rules. We proved that by having our attorney continue investigating. Mr. Colter was able to locate Tyron

Washington overseas and set up an interview. He was also able to locate the family of Len Mallard and speak to them. He has helped Mallard get into a rehab program. He then followed that up by chasing down the academic fraud information. In fact, everything you have before you today supporting that allegation, from the interviews of the players and tutors to the copied tests and interview of the individual who proctored the final exam in that course was obtained by GCSU and its attorney.

"I ask you to consider that when contemplating our case. If we get penalized for doing more than the NCAA would have done, for gathering proof that academic fraud occurred, what will be the incentive for universities to do more than sit on their hands hoping the NCAA doesn't uncover information? We all have an ethical obligation to do the right thing, but I would argue we did more than that. Punish us where we were directly at fault, but remember that this wouldn't be here before you today if we hadn't uncovered it."

Matt could tell that President Scott had the Committee's full attention. This was the moment that could backfire on them and Matt grew worried when the law professor leaned forward to push his microphone button.

"President Scott, I understand your position. I believe you do have an ethical obligation to uncover the truth even if the enforcement staff is negligent in its duty." He paused to look over at the staff. He had delivered a strong message with that comment.

The FAR continued. "I am willing to give GCSU some credit for uncovering things that might have stayed hidden if not for its efforts, but do you disagree that the fact remains that if a violation did happen, those responsible should bear the burden, even if they uncover the violation?"

"Yes sir, I agree completely with that statement," President Scott concluded. "We don't think we should receive immunity for things that happened under our watch and for the things for which we were responsible. That is not what I'm asking. What I'm asking is for the Committee to acknowledge in its findings that GCSU not only cooperated, but went much further and was diligent in uncovering much of the information. Consider that when applying a penalty. That is all we can ask."

"Does the enforcement staff have anything to add to President Scott's comments?" The Chair asked. "Do you agree that you had all but given up and only stumbled upon this information because Mr. Colter found it for you?"

"We hadn't given up," Lisa replied. "We weren't able to locate Tyron Washington or Len Mallard, but we hadn't given up. Mr. Colter interviewed the tutors and the professor who proctored the correspondence course exam without letting us know about it!"

Eyes turned to Matt. He finally weighed in.

"Let me be clear here," Matt started. "I have nothing but the utmost respect for the enforcement staff. They have a difficult job, which is sometimes made more difficult when they treat everyone, even former members of their staff like myself, as the enemy. I included Miss Lasham in the interview of Tyron Washington. He pointed us towards the fraud at the junior college. I asked Miss Lasham if she was going to gather more information regarding the correspondence course to which she replied that it wasn't needed because Mr. Washington had supplied the information."

Matt let that sink in for a minute. He could see Ed Raines looking at Lisa Lasham and shaking his head. Matt hoped he wasn't burning bridges because he would have to continue working with the enforcement staff on other cases, but it wasn't time to be timid.

"I found the paperwork that proved the tutors did most of the work and the players copied it over in their own handwriting. I confirmed that in interviews with the tutors and I chased down the professor who acknowledged his negligence in proctoring the final exam. I wasn't hiding that from the enforcement staff. The first time I was with them I handed over all of the information to them."

"Yeah, during an interview when it would have been just as easy to provide it before the interview began!" Lisa wasn't backing down, but Matt watched Ed Raines pull her back and turn off her microphone. He whispered into her ear. Her eyes got wide as she looked at him then slowly looked at the rest of the enforcement group. Whatever Ed said did the trick because Lisa slumped back into her seat and stopped talking.

"Mr. Chair," Ed Raines spoke. "We acknowledge that Mr. Colter uncovered all of this information on his own. He provided it to the enforcement staff and treated us fairly."

Everyone sat in uncomfortable silence for a minute. A minute of silence is a long time when you are sitting in a room full of people. Nobody was sure who should speak. The Chair finally asked, "is there any more discussion regarding allegation number two?"

There was none so the Chair moved on.

"Miss Lasham, would you like to introduce allegation three?"

Lisa was much more subdued. Matt felt sorry for her, but he had to remind himself that she brought this on herself and hoped it would be a learning lesson that would make her a better investigator going forward.

"Allegation number three," Lisa meekly stated. "Allegation three states that GCSU competed two ineligible players, Tyron Washington and Len Mallard, for the entire season. The two players were ineligible because of the academic fraud committed at the junior college. GCSU is responsible for this because one of its employees, Coach Ken Reid, knew about the fraud and allowed them to compete on behalf of the university. GCSU agrees to the facts and that this is a violation of NCAA rules. Mr. Reid chose not to participate in the hearing or file a written response." Lisa sat back timidly.

"Does anyone from GCSU have anything to add?" the Chair asked.

"GCSU acknowledges that Tyron Washington and Len Mallard competed while ineligible," Matt stated. "And that an employee of GCSU, Ken Reid, knew they were ineligible and was obligated under NCAA rules to share that information. He did not do that. We think it is clear that he committed the academic fraud while at the junior college and hid it from GCSU. GCSU had many educational sessions with Ken Reid and with the two players where it covered these rules, but nobody ever said a thing about it. GCSU could not have uncovered this without any suspicion so we ask the Committee to recognize that GCSU had no way to know about this or detect it and did provide the education to those involved.

"One other thing we'd like to point out," Matt continued. "GCSU did not win a game in the NCAA tournament. No additional funds were generated because of GCSU's participation in the tournament. GCSU would have received the same amount of money whether it participated in the tournament or not based on the league getting one automatic entry into the tournament and a revenue sharing formula where each school in the league shares the revenue from the NCAA basketball tournament."

Matt had discussed this point with President Scott and they both agreed that it was important to state it even though they knew the Committee would attack them a little bit on the logic. They were right.

"Mr. Colter, are you saying that GCSU had no increased revenue based on having the two ineligible players compete?" The athletics director on the Committee asked this question. Matt knew this question was coming and they had discussed having Mike Love respond to this, but President Scott had overruled and asked Matt to respond.

"We aren't saying that," Matt replied. "We are saying that no additional NCAA money was received. We readily admit that GCSU's attendance rose during the season as the team grew more successful."

"I suppose you don't happen to have those numbers?"

"Yes we do," Matt responded. "The season prior to having Tyron Washington and Len Mallard, GCSU averaged 3,500 in attendance. GCSU had fifteen home games during the season when Washington and Mallard played. The first seven games averaged 3,500 in attendance. The next three games had averaged 4,000 in attendance. During the last five games the attendance rose steadily, 4200, 4400, 4500, 4700 and finally 5000 at the final game."

Mike Love had argued against providing those numbers, but President Scott said they were going to provide anything the Committee asked and take any lumps the Committee gave out. Matt believed it would be difficult to arrive at a dollar value based solely on attendance. There were too many variables involved. Matt waited for follow up questions, but was surprised when the Chair spoke.

"Thank you Mr. Colter," the Chair spoke. "Are there any other questions regarding allegation three?"

Seeing there were none, the Chair continued. "Miss Lasham, allegation four?"

"The fourth allegation is an unethical conduct charge against Ken Reid. We had included the academic fraud committed at the junior college. Even if the Committee concludes that falls outside of NCAA jurisdiction, the unethical conduct continued when Ken Reid knowingly permitted Tyron Washington and Len Mallard to compete while ineligible. GCSU is in agreement to the facts, but leaves it to the Committee to decide whether or not this rises to an unethical conduct charge. Ken Reid chose to not participate in these proceedings and did not file a written response."

"GCSU? Do you have anything to say here?" the Chair asked.

"We agree to the facts," Matt stated. "We aren't saying that this doesn't merit a charge of unethical conduct, but we believe it is the position of the Committee to make that finding not GCSU. We have no disagreement to the NCAA allegation."

Matt thought it was important to put the allegation at the feet of the Committee and not take a hard position. The Committee would understand the logic and it might help should Ken Reid file a lawsuit against the university.

"Any questions or comments on allegation four?" the Chair asked. Seeing there were none he turned to Lisa. "Allegation five?"

"Allegation five in an institutional control charge against GCSU," Lisa stated. "The enforcement staff position is laid out in the paperwork you have received. GCSU disagrees with the allegation."

Matt could tell Lisa was a little gun shy now. He knew she realized it would be tough to reach a finding of institutional control without the first allegation. He couldn't just sit there and hope he was right.

"Committee members," Matt started. "GCSU hopes you can see that the violations committed today were the act of one person, not a university run amok. We have included in our report the education provided to the basketball staff, which is substantial. We have dates, who was involved and the subjects covered in the exhibits you have received as part of our report. We are guilty of hiring Ken Reid, but had no indication that anything was wrong with that hire. President Scott has responded to this mistake by terminating both assistant coaches and the head coach Ned McEnroe resigned when President Scott informed him that any future assistant coaches would need to have completed an advanced degree to be considered. We have taken steps to ensure this will not happen again under President Scott's leadership."

Surprisingly there were no questions. It had been only two hours, but the hearing was over. The Chair allowed for closing remarks. Ed Raines said the staff agreed that GCSU had made a mistake, but had learned from it. He gave GCSU high marks for not only cooperating, but often leading the NCAA in the investigation.

President Scott thanked the Committee for its time and apologized for being the reason they had to take that time. He told them he had learned quite a bit from the hearing and would be a better president because of it. That scored high marks with the Committee by the looks on their faces.

The Chair concluded the hearing by explaining that the Committee would begin deliberations, arrive at a conclusion then take time to write a formal report. The normal time from the conclusion of the hearing to the formal written notification of the findings was six to eight weeks. He thanked everyone for their participation and closed the hearing.

Matt shook President Scott's hand then allowed him to speak with Committee members. Mat walked over to the NCAA table. He spoke with a few of the directors who greeted him warmly. He was happy to see they took no offense. One of them did say that it was a tough lesson for Lisa to learn, but they hoped she would be better because of it. Another joked that Matt would not be getting any invitations to future NCAA parties.

Matt finally arrived at Ed's seat.

"I hope I wasn't too rough," Matt said.

"No, not in the least," Ed replied warmly. "You did what you needed to do for your client. Not only that, but you warned me in advance. I can see that I should have been much more involved in this case."

"Perhaps I should have called you to tell you what was going on, but I'm in a difficult place where I don't want to be seen as tattling on an enforcement staff member. Besides, who am I? And why would anyone believe me?" Matt asked.

"Don't sell yourself short," Ed stated. "You gained more respect today because you were able to set aside friendships and do what you believed to be right. Maybe you could go talk to Lisa and try to mend some fences?"

Matt thanked Ed and walked over to where Lisa was packing her belongings.

"Lisa, you don't have to say anything to me," Matt said. "I know I'm not your favorite person right now, but I think you have a lot of potential and I hope we can work together again."

Without looking at Matt she mumbled, "so you can beat me up again?"

"No, I'm serious," Matt replied. "You have a lot of great qualities, but you need to realize that not everyone is dishonest. Sometimes dishonest people work with others who are honest. Don't throw everyone in the same pool. I will help you all I can if you work with me, but when you make me the enemy you have to realize that it makes your job tougher. One of the most important skills is learning who you can trust. Sometimes you have no way to know, but other times you need to rely on the experience of others. Ed would have told you I can be trusted. I do hope we can work together and no hard feelings?"

Matt put forth his hand. Lisa eyed him wearily. Finally she shook his hand.

"You really did beat me up today, but I'll do better next time."

"I'm sure you will," Matt smiled. "Between you and me, the directors and especially Ed hold you in very high regards. They all made mistakes along the way, but the good ones learn from them."

Matt and Lisa parted. Matt spoke to many of the Committee members who praised him and the defense, but all spoke very highly of President Scott. The Chair pulled Matt aside and told him that the Committee would benefit from having President Scott as a member and asked Matt to encourage him to consider it when there was an opening on the Committee.

Matt drove to the airport with a very happy GCSU group. They parted company with Matt telling them that they would talk in the weeks leading up the release of the findings.

Matt finally relaxed waiting for his plane. That had gone just about as perfectly as he could have hoped. He was pretty confident that GCSU would escape serious sanctions, but six to eight weeks is a long time to wait!

CHAPTER TWENTY TWO

During the next seven weeks Matt spoke often with President Scott. They talked about what they could have done better, but Matt was at a loss because he thought it had gone just about as perfectly as he could have hoped.

President Scott began the search for a head basketball coach and asked Matt to find out any information he could about four or five specific candidates. GCSU hired a young, up and coming coach, who was excited for the opportunity. GCSU knew that if he was successful he would receive, and probably take, a bigger job. President Scott was okay with that.

"There are the big fish who pay the most, then there are the little fish who hope to do their best and be successful. We can't pay as much so we know that when we are successful we are going to watch our people move on to bigger things. That is the way of life for a mid-major program like ours."

Matt had thought about that often and agreed with President Scott. "The only exception to that is when you find a coach who likes it where he is and knows he makes enough money to be happy. The Gonzagas and Butlers of the world are few and far between, but that is the rare exception that allows a mid-major, and I hate that term, to be successful for a longer period of time."

Finally the day arrived when GCSU received notification that the Committee on Infraction ruling would be made public. GCSU received the actual report just a short time before the Chair of the Committee held a press conference to announce the findings.

For a school like GCSU, the press conference wasn't much. If it had been a basketball power like Kentucky, UCLA or Indiana, it would have been major news, but GCSU was able to escape barely noticed by those outside of its small community.

Matt read through the report and finally came to the penalties. GCSU was put on probation for two years, which is the minimum standard for major cases. The basketball program lost two official visits. Official visits are when a university pays for a prospect and his parents to visit the school to see if it might be a place where he wants to attend school and play. They are important, but losing two official visits wouldn't hurt at all.

The new basketball staff was mandated to meet with the compliance staff at GCSU weekly for the first year. Matt actually liked that and thought it would help Shawn Morgan develop a better relationship with the staff. President Scott agreed and thought he would start having all sports have weekly compliance meetings with Shawn Morgan.

The really major penalty was that Ken Reid received a lifetime show cause penalty, which meant that if he ever had any desire to coach again at an NCAA school, the school that was interested in hiring him would need to show to the Committee why it shouldn't receive a penalty for hiring him. What this really meant, was that while it wasn't impossible for Reid to ever coach at an NCAA school again, it would be very difficult and he would have to walk through all of these violations again with his new school prior to employment.

There were no penalties levied against Randy Culp or Ned McEnroe. The last Matt heard McEnroe had finally retired from coaching and was doing some commentary for ESPN. Culp had been hired at a junior college in Wyoming, which Matt thought would need to be watched, but not by him. It might not be the last time he encountered Randy Culp.

When Matt spoke with President Scott he found out that President Scott was very pleased with the results. President Scott thanked Matt then surprised him by asking if Matt ever had any desire to work on a campus.

"Not really, I'm pretty happy doing what I do, but why do you ask?"

"I haven't announced anything yet," President Scott replied. "But Mike Love will be resigning after this academic year to pursue other opportunities."

"Really?" Matt asked. "What is he leaving to do?"

"He doesn't know yet," President Scott stated. "Watching him during the investigation and hearing helped me realize I didn't know him as well as I should have. I'm just not comfortable with him leading our athletics department so I told him I would support him and give him a good recommendation, but that I thought it was time to go in a different direction."

Inwardly Matt agreed, but he would have never said that to President Scott. The way the court system worked these days, Matt always had to be on guard against being sued. Matt knew someone who might be perfect for GCSU so he gave President Scott the name and contact information.

They parted on good terms. Matt had come to appreciate President Scott. Outwardly he could be whatever he needed to be, cowboy to some, a businessman to others. Matt knew that inside was a keen mind that grasped things quickly and a man of high morals.

Matt called Ced Booker to let him know the results.

"That is better than you could have hoped for," Ced stated after hearing the penalties. "Was GCSU ecstatic about the findings?"

"They were pretty happy," Matt replied. "We have another great reference if we need it. Now on to more important things, how is Len Mallard doing in rehab?"

Ced chuckled. "It was pretty rough at the start. Len tried to sneak out a time or two, but then Shirly Jo got more involved. She took a little time off of work and went to the rehab facility. She convinced them to let her work there for a week without pay in exchange for being able to sleep and eat there. Len straightened up right away. He just finished his time and was offered a job at the rehab center. He is very excited to be able to help others for a change instead of needing help."

"Well that's great," Matt stated. "Do you think it will last?"

"You should see him Matt, he is a completely different person. You wouldn't recognize him if you knew him from a couple of months ago. He told me he was always focused on himself, only caring about what he could get out of something, be it money, power or whatever. He said now he realizes what his mom actually represents and has found his calling in helping others. I actually think he not only will stick, but he will be very good in this. As part of his employment he is going back to school. He has definitely turned his life around."

"That makes me feel better than anything else that came out of this case," Matt stated. "Thanks Ced for suggesting we pay for it."

"No problem, that is what we do!"

"Sometimes, that is what we do, when we are lucky to be in the right place at the right time!"

"True enough," Ced responded. "Are you going to let Holly know the outcome? She always likes to hear a good ending."

"Yes I'll let her know and I may have more work heading your way. I got a call earlier this morning from a very prominent football player. He wouldn't go into details, but I believe he is in a mess of trouble and is trying to figure a way out. I'll let you know once I know more, but this is going to be major news so I'm going to need all the help you can muster."

"Looking forward to it," Ced replied. "Working with you is never dull!"

Matt hung up the phone feeling happy that Len Mallard had turned his life around. Matt enjoyed making a positive difference in people's lives. There are a lot of people in the sports world who use their fame and/or money to help others, but there aren't a lot who do it quietly with no publicity for themselves. Matt had to admit he liked being one of those people.

Another case concluded, mine fields avoided and a positive outcome. Matt wished they all went like this, but the next one would prove they don't!

Thank you for reading my book. If you would like to hear more stories about college sports scandals look for future books in the Matt Colter series of books by Ron Barker

If you are interested in having Ron Barker speak to your company or group or book him on your podcast or radio show you can contact him via his website at

www.ronaldbarkersa.wixsite.com/website

Made in the USA
Middletown, DE
20 April 2022

64527000R00089